David and the Drainosaurs

Tales of the Teleporting Topsider
(Book 1)

Written & Illustrated by
Janyce Brawn

Published by
Dragonfly Publishing, Inc.

DAVID AND THE DRAINOSAURS

Tales of the Teleporting Topsider (Book 1)

Juvenile Fantasy
Rated G for all audiences
Released in 2021

Paperback Edition
EAN 978-1-941278-89-5 | ISBN 1-941278-89-2

Hardback Edition
EAN 978-1-941278-90-1 | ISBN 1-941278-90-6

eBook Edition
EAN 978-1-941278-91-8 | ISBN 1-941278-91-4

Story Text & Illustrations ©2021 Janyce Brawn
Dragonfly Logo ©2001 Terri Branson

Published in the United States of America by
Dragonfly Publishing, Inc.
Website: www.dragonflypubs.com

Acknowledgements

Thanks to the help of my critique group, Fellowship of the Quill, who have tirelessly read each page and trouped through all of David's adventures with me. Also, thanks to the encouragement from my family and friends who read the book and answered questions. Thanks to my husband, Lyn, for all his computer help when I was ready to scream when issues arose. I especially thank Babs who opened doors for me, and Terri who is a formatting whiz, for all her work in bringing this book to fruition.

Dedication

I'd like to dedicate this book to two of my youngest readers, Kiley and Giana. Thank you for your enthusiasm and excitement to read more about David and his adventures.

Cast of Characters

David Gonzales
Luis Gonzales
Oliver the Ferret
Princess Doris Drainosaurus
King of the Drainosaurs
Captain Scarlet of the Drainosaurs
Herman the Hermit Crab
Grandpappy Hunstable the Hermit Crab
Red Hair-Ring the Troll
Blister the Troll
Stool Pigeons Brutus and Portia
Prince Alexander of Plumberia
King Thomas Rose of Plumberia
Winston the Ostrich
Princess Ardis of the Rose Mountain Fairies
Prince Klaus of the Rose Mountain Fairies
King of the Rose Mountain Fairies
Fairy Prime Minister Reardon

and

Gert and Trudy, the Two-headed
Psychedelic Caterpillar/Butterfly

CHAPTER 1

MAMA didn't realize babysitting Luis was the worst job in the world.

There he was, holding Abuela's ring that she had left to Mama. I knew how much Mama treasured it, and I wished Luis understood. I ground my teeth together. If he loses it while I'm watching him, I'll be in trouble. He blames me for everything. First, the broken garage window when we were playing baseball, and *he* threw the ball at it, and now this.

I sneaked up behind Luis. "Put. That. Back," I whispered.

Luis jumped. "David, I'm not hurting it." He put Mama's ring on a little red and orange sombrero-shaped ring dish at the corner of the sink. The ring's yellow diamonds winked in the sunlight. "There."

"Scram!" I grabbed a placemat decorated with red chili peppers off the kitchen table and tossed it at him. I missed.

Luis picked it up from the floor and threw it back like a discus.

I ducked and the placemat landed on the little dish. I yanked it off and gasped as Mama's ring tumbled into the sink.

"No!" I tried to catch the ring, but it disappeared.

"Ooh, you're in trouble now," said Luis.

"You started it. I hate babysitting you! I wish I was out with my friends." I clenched and unclenched my fists.

"I'm going to tell," Luis chanted. "I'm going to tell."

"Don't even try." I reached for him as he ran out the backdoor, but all I caught was air. "Better keep quiet!"

Luis laughed as the door slammed.

My stomach did somersaults, and my mouth tasted bitter. I had to get Mama's ring. I just had to!

After I turned twelve, Mama decided that I was old enough to babysit, when she and Papa weren't home.

"Just think of how much Luis looks up to you, David," Mama had said the other day. "Play with him. If your roles were reversed, you'd want him to play with you."

I knew what she meant, but she didn't know how bratty Luis was. I wished I could do what I wanted, instead of being stuck with him.

Turning back to the sink, I noticed the air shimmering with tiny swirling dots. Curious, I tiptoed over and peered into the drain.

Mama's ring hadn't fallen through the metal crosspiece at the bottom. It sat on top of a piece of carrot. We didn't have a garbage disposal, so sometimes pieces of food stuck there.

Jabbing a couple of fingers down to get it, I poked something warm and squishy climbing up through the drain.

"Watch it!" a high-pitched voice commanded.

I squeaked, yanking back my hand.

Shocked, I stared at a green finger-length glob with thin arms and a large reptile head on a long, thick neck. Beady black eyes glared. Tiny ears wiggled. Three claw-like fingers, wearing gold rings, balled into fists and shook at me. Its fat, dress-covered belly jiggled. It looked like a weird dinosaur in clothing.

"How rude," it said in a huff. "Don't you know not to poke at strangers?"

The air sparkled.

I blinked, but the strange creature still stared at me. My hand shook as I pointed in the drain. "I d-d-dropped Mama's ring down there. I have to get it back."

"Well, I haven't seen it, I'm sure." The miniature dinosaur straddled the holes in the drain, hands planted on the sides of her big belly.

"Unreal," I muttered. "I'm talking to a dinosaur in the drain."

"Drainosaur."

"What?"

"We're called Drainosaurs." She shrugged. "We live in the kingdom of Drainovia. I'm Princess Doris Drainosaurus. Now, hurry up and describe this ring you're talking about, so you can leave me alone."

"It's a gold ring with three diamonds. It was right there a minute ago on a piece of carrot."

Princess Doris Drainosaurus swiveled her head, looking around the drain. "It's not here, so I guess you're mistaken. Well, goodbye." She reached behind to pick up the round chunk of carrot and placed it on her head like a hat. The ring was wedged on top of it.

"Hey! There's the ring." I reached for it.

"No!" Princess Doris' fingers clamped onto the carrot and ring. "It's the missing crown of Drainovia. We've been looking for it, since the end of the Plumberian War. Now that I've found it, I've got to give it to the king." She moved to the other side of the drain, making the air shimmer.

"Wait!" I shoved in two fingers, hooked the ring, and tugged.

The next thing I knew, I began to shrink. I grabbed for the faucet with my other hand but it hit the handle and water started to drip down on me. "Aiii!" I screamed.

Fear knotted in my stomach. I became smaller and smaller, until the sink surrounded me. The faucet towered over me with water dribbling out. My breath caught in my throat, as water splashed over me.

I lost my balance and toppled through the drain. My feet pushed the squishy drainosaur, and we slid out of control.

"Help!" I tried to grab the wall of the pipe. All I could feel was cold gooey slime ooze between my fingers. I kicked at the sides, but my feet flew up. I slid down on my back like I was riding on a wild, dark, water slide. I felt like throwing up.

The walls slapped us with slithery tendrils of gunk. With a *whoosh* we tumbled past the trap and slid into a horizontal pipe. A light flashed, blinding me for a moment.

The drainosaur squashed me against the side of the pipe. Struggling to breathe, I gulped a lungful of air that smelled like rotten eggs and onions.

I shoved Princess Doris. "Move," I grunted.

She rolled off.

I stood up in a little bit of water that continued to flow through the pipe ahead of us. We were way under the sink, maybe close to the sewer line. Dark walls surrounded us. Purple slime pulsed like something out of a scary movie. What was going to happen next? As I shook off the water, cold smelly gunk dripped from my hair into my eyes.

"Gross." I wiped it off. "Get up, Princess. I want my mother's ring back. Now."

As she struggled to her feet, Princess Doris tugged her carrot-hat tight to her head. The ring still stuck to the top. "I told you, this isn't your ring." She glanced around. Her eyes bulged, and she trembled. "You've pushed us down into Plumberian territory. We've got to get out of here before the Plumberians find us. Hold on."

The princess grabbed my hand. The drain wall swirled around, making me dizzy. Soon we stood in the trap, where the slime was not as thick. Above us shone a tiny pinpoint of light. Hope lifted my spirits. Maybe I could crawl out after all. I touched the wall.

It was too slippery to climb with water still dribbling down. I hoped Luis stayed out of trouble until I got back—with Mama's ring.

"Whew, that was close," said Princess Doris. "What were you thinking? The Plumberians would love to capture me and you. Humph. You're from above. They would really like to question a topsider to pry out your secrets. I don't care how mistaken you are about my crown.

Nobody deserves to be caught and forced to live in their old-fashioned conditions." Princess Doris' bottom lip quivered. Wiping slime from her orange dress, she kicked a rainbow-colored pile of strange vegetable-shaped hats toward me. "Here, you'd better wear one of these to get back home." She touched her carrot-hat with the diamond ring and disappeared.

"Wait!" I gaped. Where had she gone? I spun around. My gaze fell on the pile of vegetable hats. What had she meant? How could a hat help me get home? I swallowed my sour tasting panic and picked up a green-bean shaped hat, setting it on my head. The strap fit snug under my chin. How was I going to get back Mama's ring? How could I get out of here? Maybe it was all a dream. I pinched myself. "Ouch."

Great. Now what? I needed to get out of there and get back to my normal size.

A small sign near the pile of hats read: *Drainovia Door One. Push.*

I pushed on the cold, slippery, metal surface. Goo melted at my touch. As the door fell flat, I stumbled forward, landing on my face a few inches from the edge of the door. Above and around me was clear blue sky.

The door tilted and I struggled to hold on. My legs slid sideways.

"Help!" I shrieked.

CHAPTER 2

THE door righted itself.

Scrambling to sit, I gasped at the sight of dozens of brightly clothed drainosaurs sitting on flying doors. They zoomed all around me. A faint lemony breeze blew in my face, stiffening some of the slime that still clung to the ends of my hair.

Leather straps slid from the sides of the door, shot up, and hooked around my waist.

"Welcome to Drainovia," a metallic voice said below me. "Your destination, please."

A click echoed, and the door unlatched from the edge of the pipe. Another door magically took its place.

"Uh, find Princess Doris Drainosaurus," I said.

The nearest drainosaur looked at me and grunted. Below I spied a town of pink square block buildings surrounded by neat grassy plots. All had narrow windows facing the streets. Several windowless blue cylindrical buildings swayed from side-to-side, sometimes even changing in height. They reminded me of a springy coil toy. A large building with circular towers on each corner dominated the center of the town. Lemon trees dotted the landscape. Green drainosaurs jostled each other through the streets. Distant water shimmered in the sunlight.

I pointed to a sparkle on an orange-hatted drainosaur. "There she is, entering the tallest cylinder."

My door zoomed down to land beside others lined up in a parking lot. Then the leather straps unhooked from around me.

"Thanks," I said.

I dashed into the building labeled *Drainovia Royal Ministry of Stairs and Records.*

My eyes had to adjust to the cool dimness. Occasionally, flashes of color would explode, and I could see dozens of stairs in all colors of the rainbow. Each was numbered. There were wide, narrow, short, and tall sets of stairs. Some swung from side-to-side, while others changed from stairs to ramps and then back to stairs.

"Wow," I whispered. "What kind of place is this?"

"Whom are you here to see?" a shrill voice called.

I looked around. No one else was in the building.

"Over here," the voice said again. "You've come to meet someone, haven't you? Where is your pass?" A light radiated down from the tall ceiling, illuminating a large book which sat on the floor in the middle of the room. Its pages waved.

I walked over and looked down at it.

At the top of the page an old, lined face with beady eyes peered at me. The eyes blinked, as thin lips moved at the bottom of the page. "What are you waiting for?"

I jumped back. "You're t-talking."

"Of course, I'm talking." The face at the top of the page rolled its eyes at me. "I'm here to tell you what you need to know."

"I never saw a talking book before." I bent over to examine it. "I'm looking for Princess Doris."

"Well, show me your pass."

"Pass? I don't have a pass," I replied with a sigh. "But I just talked to the Princess a few minutes ago."

"This is highly irregular. Wait just a moment, as I check regulations." The book's musty pages flipped back and forth with a soft whir. "Ah, page 603, paragraph 4. Hmm. Here. It says: 'When having spoken with royalty and on their recommendation, a guest may enter the royal chambers and send the royal secretary back to the Room of Stairs and Records with a written pass.' So do it and be quick."

I glanced around. "Okay. Uh, which stairs?"

The eyes squinted at me. "The gold stairs, Number 71. Hurry now. The Princess is very busy planning the ceremony, you know."

"What ceremony?"

"Tomorrow Princess Doris officially takes over the Kingdom of Drainovia." The eyes stared at me. "The old king is going on a vacation. About time, too, I might add. He's needed one ever since the end of the Plumberian War. Since the crown was stolen, everything has gotten worse. Are you sure you talked to Princess Doris? Hmm. Do *you* know anything about the crown?"

"Me?" I squeaked, staggering back a few steps. "Of course not." I tried to stare down the book's accusing glare.

"Well, be on your way then. Make sure the royal secretary brings me your pass." The book closed its eyes and sighed.

I looked around the room. "Where are the gold stairs?"

"Behind you, on the left, Number 71. Hurry." The book snapped shut, and the light above dimmed.

"Gold stairs. Number 71," I muttered to myself.

As if hearing its number, the stairs pulsed with a soft golden glow drawing me to it.

It figured. Number 71 had to be the longest one in the room.

Once I reached the top of the stairs, I leaned against the railing to catch my breath. Now what?

As if reading my thoughts, far below me the book flipped open. "Don't forget to touch your hat!" it shouted.

I touched my green bean hat. A door with a fancy knob appeared. I opened the door into a big room with crystal lights that sparkled off highly polished furniture. The lemon fragrance smacked me full force.

A group of drainosaurs turned from their discussions to stare at me.

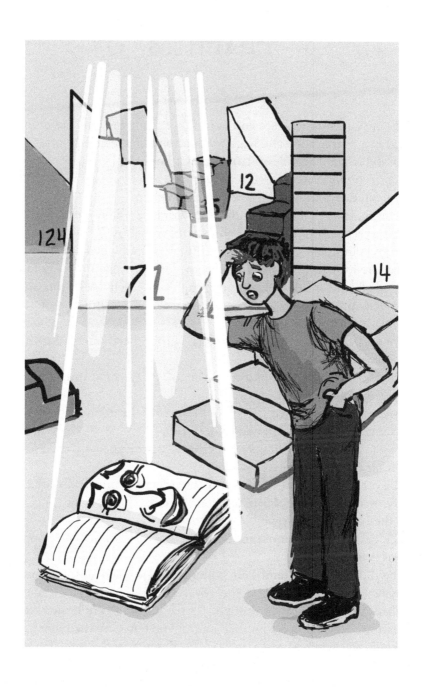

CHAPTER 3

"WHO are you, and why are you here?" asked a large wrinkled drainosaur dressed in a purple robe and leaning on a sparkling jeweled staff.

I stood straight and cleared my throat. "I'm David Gonzales. I've come from the top world to see Princess Doris on a very important matter."

The old drainosaurs whispered to each other.

"Hmm. Have a seat, David," the wrinkled drainosaur said. "Help yourself to some lemons. Keeps you sharp, you know."

From behind him a scarlet-robed drainosaur frowned at me.

Scattered throughout the room were clusters of lemons in gold bowls on round tables. One drainosaur sat at each table peeling a lemon, and then breaking it into sections to be passed around. The drainosaurs sucked noisily with puckered lips.

Princess Doris entered from a door across the room. "What are you doing here?"

I jumped off the chair and ran over to her. "I came to talk about my mother's diamond ring."

Princess Doris crossed her arms. "I'm sorry. I can't help you."

"But you have it." I pointed to her head.

"What I have is the Drainovian crown," said Princess Doris.

"But it isn't your crown!"

The other drainosaurs stopped sucking their lemons and stared at me.

The scarlet-robed drainosaur plodded over, his eyes bulging. "Why, this *is* the Drainovian crown!"

The rest of the drainosaurs thundered across the room, stopping in front of Princess Doris.

The old wrinkled drainosaur pounded his jeweled staff on the floor. "As King, I officially declare the royal Drainovian crown found." He scratched his chin. "I never thought I'd see it again." He leaned closer to me. "Hmm. You're not a Plumberian, but you could be their spy trying to take our crown again. Maybe you work for them. Yes, that's it." He pointed his jeweled staff at me. "Cuffs, seize him. Take him to the High Tower."

A pair of winged handcuffs rose from a shelf by the door and clinked as they flew across the room. They clasped tightly around my hands.

"You can't do this!" I yelled. "Princess Doris, you know I'm right!"

Princess Doris turned away.

The scarlet-robed drainosaur took charge. "I'm Captain Scarlet of the Drainovian Police and Armed Forces. Be quiet and follow me."

As the winged handcuffs dragged me out another door, I twisted and tried to shake my hands free. Scraping and bumping up a dark, narrow set of stone steps, I watched my hat tumble down to wedge behind the door at the bottom. I struggled, pulling my wrists against the biting metal cuffs.

"Noooo!" Tears burned my eyes. My hope of returning home had rolled away like my hat.

Captain Scarlet stopped at the top of the steps and took a large silver key from a hook beside a metal door. He opened the door, and then put the key back on the hook.

The handcuffs pulled me into a huge circular stone-walled room. In front of a window sat a plain wooden desk with two straight-backed chairs. Next to them was a screen with a cot on the other side. At a command from the captain, the handcuffs released me and flew outside. The door slammed shut behind them.

The captain moved to the desk and motioned for me to sit in a chair across from him. He took a pen and paper from deep within his robe. "Well, I'll give you a minute, so state your case."

"I don't belong here," I blurted, leaning toward the desk. The chair tipped forward and I toppled to the floor.

"Yes, I can see that. The question is *why* are you here?" The captain frowned, looking down at me. He tapped the pen on the desk.

I scrambled back onto the chair. "I fell down my kitchen sink drain, when I tried to get my mother's diamond ring. You have to believe me. Please let me go. I'm supposed to be home to take care of my little brother. He needs me." Cold sweat beaded on my forehead.

Captain Scarlet narrowed his eyes. "Hmm." He bent and scribbled something on the paper. "You will have to stay here, while I investigate your claim. The door locks, so don't try to escape. Food will be brought to you three times a day." His chair scraped on the floor, as he rose. He folded the paper, tucked it in a pocket, and then walked to the door.

"But I can't stay here. I have to go home. This is all a mistake!"

The door shut with a clang.

CHAPTER 4

"WHEW," squeaked a tiny voice. "I thought he'd never leave."

I whirled around.

A little ferret dressed in a pair of overalls climbed out from under the cot. He dusted off his paws and wiggled his whiskers.

"Who are you?" I asked.

"My name is Oliver. And you?"

"I'm David Gonzales. What are you doing here?"

"I was looking for a little food for my family, when I got caught and arrested in the royal kitchen. You wouldn't have any food, would you? They seem to have forgotten me. I've been here long enough to know that even though Captain Scarlet has a desk here, he rarely uses it. He allowed me to write a letter home yesterday. Lucky for me, you're here now. Uh, about that food?" Oliver licked his lips and held out a paw.

I reached in my pocket and pulled out a beef stick that I had put in there this morning when I got dressed. "Here." I broke off a piece and handed it to him.

"Ah, just what I need." Oliver bit into it. "So you lost your mother's ring and fell down the drain. What's the big deal? You've got three days to get back home before you're stuck here forever. Easy." He swallowed and took another bite.

"Not really. They think my mother's ring is the Drainovian Crown. Princess Doris took off with it, and I followed." I paced back and forth clenching and unclenching my hands. "I have to get the ring back and go home." I whirled around to face Oliver. "Wait. What do you mean I'll be stuck here forever?"

Oliver wiped his mouth and whiskers. "They say that things or people that fall into Drainovia have three days to return before they become permanent. Some strange and funny things have fallen down here and stayed. They're stored in a room at the top of one of the stairs in the *Drainovia Royal Ministry of Stairs and Records.*"

The ferret tugged at his whiskers. "If they think your ring is our crown, no wonder they put you in here. The crown has been missing for almost a year. They thought the Stool Pigeons stole it for the Plumberians during the war. The crown is linked to some story about prosperity. There's a lot of trouble now because it's gone, and we certainly ain't prosperous. I lost my job and that's why I tried to get some food here. The king eats well no matter what. Food is scarce for everyone else. What little we do have is pretty expensive, too."

"You think you've got trouble? That's nothing, if I don't get back Mama's ring." Sitting down on the cot, I ran my hand through my hair.

Oliver smiled at me. "But now that you're here, I have an idea."

"What is it?" I asked with doubt.

"You see that window in the door? Well, you lift me up to it, so I can wiggle through. I can't get to it by myself, since the walls and door are too smooth. Then I'll shimmy up the plumbing to the key beside the door and use it to get you out. It's a fool-proof plan." Oliver grinned, strutting around me with his paws hooked into the straps of his overalls.

"What about the Cuffs? Captain Scarlet said they'd be outside the door."

"Oh, yeah, let me think." Oliver twitched his tail. "I wish I had a teleporting hat. They're the best form of transportation in Drainovia. They took mine, when I was arrested. Looks like you don't have one either."

"I had a hat, but it rolled behind the door at the bottom of the stairs when they dragged me up here." I sighed, looking at the desk. "Maybe Captain Scarlet will discover I'm telling the truth and let me go. He has to! I've got to get Mama's ring and go home. This is the first day of my three days, right? He can't take that long to discover I'm telling the truth."

"Don't count on it. The drainosaurs are a selfish lot. They'll use your mother's ring for their own purposes. With Princess Doris becoming the Queen, the crown would make her popular with the drainosaurs." Oliver walked back and forth, scratching his chin with one paw.

"You know, that Captain Scarlet is a real strange one. He makes my whiskers twitch. We have to get out by ourselves. Hmm. If I remember right, the Cuffs sleep until they are ordered into service, so it should be easy to get by them. I guess when I get through the window, I'll just have to scoot down the stairs and find your hat. Once under it, I can think about being in here with you and I'll be back before you know it. Then you can wear the hat and get us both out of here." Oliver jumped up and down, clapping his paws. "Yes! That's perfect."

I stood up and cracked my knuckles. "Are you sure you'll come back for me?"

"On my honor." Oliver crossed his heart. "We ferrets help others, 'cause we know what it's like to be the underdog—er, ferret in this case.

Besides, you fed me and it's your hat. It uses our thoughts to move us into another place."

"Will those hats take us anywhere we want to go?"

"Most of the time. The hats have a thought-converter teleporting machine inside them. I studied them in Basic Machine class when I was in school. They were great to use to stay out of trouble. Yeah, I've had some fine hats."

"You went to school? Do all animals in Drainovia talk and go to school?"

"Yeah, if we're lucky. You have to pass a test at the end. I passed with flying colors. I got a blue and yellow starred diploma." Oliver smiled, and then climbed on my shoulder. "Okay, let's go."

"You're sure this will work?" I turned to look into his dark eyes.

He twitched his nose. "What have we got to lose?"

I tiptoed to the door and held Oliver in my hand next to the window.

"Here," I whispered. "Be careful but be fast."

Oliver wiggled his body between the bars and was gone.

CHAPTER 5

I peered through the window and watched Oliver scurry down the steps until he disappeared. There was a little scratching sound, and then silence. As I waited, the Cuffs never moved.

Oliver cleared his throat.

I whirled to see Oliver climb out of my hat on the floor behind me.

"That was easy. Now let's get out of here. There was a celebration goin' on in the Royal chamber, so they'll never miss us. At least not yet."

I set my hat on my head and picked up Oliver. "Okay, where do we go now?"

"First we need to get you a disguise. You stick out like a sore paw. Here, I'll think and you hold on." Oliver climbed under the hat and poked out his head. "Ready?"

I nodded.

Oliver's back claws dug into my scalp, as he tried to keep his balance. "A simple yes, would've worked fine."

"Ouch! Yes."

Suddenly, the room blurred, and little dots and swirls of color surrounded us. My head spun and my stomach heaved.

When the colors stopped, we were on a busy street with all kinds of stalls in a market place. I grabbed the rough wooden planks on the side of the nearest stall to steady myself.

"Didn't you close your eyes when we traveled?" Oliver *tsked-tsked* at me. "Well, you've been initiated into the Hat Riders the hard way. Lesson number one: always close your eyes when traveling between points. The only time you look where you're going is when you just touch your hat to make special doors appear. I'll sit under your hat and peek out while you walk a bit."

Drainosaurs and other strange creatures bumped into me and the smells of fried foods reminded me of fairs at home. My mouth watered as I made my way past a couple stalls selling lemonade and sausage with fried onions and peppers. "Oliver, I thought you said food was scarce?"

"It is. We used to have dozens of stalls selling all kinds of food. Now there are just two, and their prices are way more than many can afford.

Most places sell toys, jewelry, and clothing."

A fat wrinkly drainosaur selling green vests and pants blocked my way. "You need a vest? Pants? I have the best prices." The drainosaur rubbed his claw-like fingers together, leaning closer. His greedy eyes shone as he looked at my blue jeans and t-shirt.

"Uh, uh," I stammered.

"How about a trade?" Oliver's high voice offered.

The drainosaur looked at me strangely.

"What do you have in your pockets?" Oliver whispered.

I reached into my pockets and pulled out a hockey puck, a key, a pen knife, a couple of quarters, a rubber band, a small magnifying glass, and the rest of the beef stick.

"Trade this black circle for a vest and pants with suspenders, biggest you've got and two green pillows," said Oliver.

"What good is it?" The drainosaur poked the puck in my hand. "I never saw it before. How do I know you aren't cheating me?"

"Here, I'll show you." I put everything else back in my pocket and set the hockey puck on the dirt in front of the stall. I spotted a stick and hit the puck back and forth. "You aim at a net or, here, this old can will work." I shot the puck into an empty coffee can on the ground across from the stall. "Goal! See, it's a game you can play."

"I like that. Okay, you get vest, pants, and two pillows. I get black circle, stick, and can. Rest you keep. I make fair deals." The drainosaur smiled a broken-toothed grin.

Standing to the side and trying to avoid curious stares, I took the clothes and put them on top of my jeans and t-shirt. There was room for the pillows.

"Take that long skinny green pillow and that big fat one," Oliver whispered.

I grabbed the two pillows and said goodbye to the drainosaur.

Oliver giggled. "Put the fat pillow under the vest and in the pants so you look like a drainosaur."

"Is this supposed to be my tail?" I squeezed the long pillow.

"Yeah, let's go to the jewelry store to get some pins. Good thing you have topside money."

Dodging drainosaurs, we headed to a nearby stall. The drainosaur in charge was a young female wearing a long red dress.

"Can I help you?" She smiled. Big gold hoop earrings glittered from her tiny ears.

"I'd like a couple of simple pins." I set a quarter on the counter.

"Well, how about these?" She pointed to a tray of long silver pins.

I picked out two and gave her the money.

Oliver shifted under the hat. "Go into that alley between those two stalls ahead on the right."

A few minutes later, tail attached, I swung into the street and bumped into the side of Captain Scarlet.

His long tail flicked me away, as he rushed past carrying a large cage. Two squawking pigeons flopped from side-to-side.

CHAPTER 6

I pulled my hat as far down my face as I could without losing Oliver. Little dots and swirls of color surrounded us. I felt dizzy and sick again.

"Whew, that was close!" Oliver squealed, as he pushed up my hat.

"Ooh," I groaned.

"Sorry, we didn't have much choice on that trip. We'll have to work out a signal, or I'll just tug at your hair. You'll get the hang of it soon."

I swallowed to keep from vomiting. "Just tug my hair, please. Do you think Captain Scarlet recognized me?"

"I think we're safe for now. Captain Scarlett wasn't looking at you. But, boy, those Stool Pigeons are in trouble!"

We were at the edge of the city on a grassy hill covered with lemon trees and dandelions. Water shone on a sandy beach below us. The air smelled of salt and lemons. I eased down onto the grass, using my tail pillow as a soft seat. I took off my hat, and Oliver slid into my lap.

Puffy pale-peach clouds floated far above on a soft breeze in a bright blue sky. A bee buzzed on a nearby dandelion. Birds chirped. Back in the city a whistle blew.

Oliver rolled a blade of grass between his paws. "The last pair of Stool Pigeons that the Captain caught worked for the Plumberians. We think they flew the coop with our crown."

"If we find them and get the crown, I can trade it for my mother's ring. Exactly where would the Stool Pigeons go?"

"Probably to Plumberia. See that?" Oliver pointed across the sea. "That's Plumberia at the base of Rose Mountain." He yawned and stretched. "I sure could use a nap. There are lots of caves around the coast. Let's hide in one. I don't think anybody will find us there."

"If I don't have long to stay here, shouldn't we go to Plumberia to get the crown? And I thought you'd be leaving to go back to your family by now." I grabbed my hat, rolled on my stomach, and pushed up to stand.

"We'll have to scout out the crown. The Plumberians won't just hand it over. By the way, my wife takes the kids to her mother's when I go foraging for food. They're happy to get away. I won't need to be back 'til tomorrow or the next day. Besides, I'm all for an adventure. Keeps me on my toes. Anyway, you might need my help." Oliver scrambled to the top of my head. "Now, let's get to the cave." He settled under my hat, but poked his head out. "Go down the hill to the beach and turn right. See that pile of rocks? The cave is just past them, where the water has dug a hole into the bank."

We plodded down the hill. The pillows and extra clothing made me sweat. The sea looked cool and clear. Maybe I could take a swim. I practically ran toward the water.

Oliver's claws dug into my scalp. "Whoa! What's the rush? Yikes!"

He jumped off as we tumbled over a small cliff. The pillows cushioned my fall onto the sandy beach.

I grabbed my hat and brushed sand off my vest, pillows, and pants. "Oliver, where are you?"

"Here."

The smell made me gag even before I found him beside a big pile of dead fish, eyeball to eye socket with one near the water. They were mostly bones, but some were still rotting with flies buzzing around.

I held my tail pillow over my nose. "Whew! Are you okay? Let's get out of here."

As we scrambled away, my shoe caught on a stone sticking up from the sand. I tripped and fell headfirst again.

I grabbed the jagged stone, ready to toss it into the water, but stopped as I noticed strange symbols scratched on it.

"The crown can be found where Halibut abound," Oliver translated. "A case is closed on a scarlet rose."

"Do you think it means the Drainovian crown?" I brushed some dirt off the edge of the stone.

"That's the only crown missing. It's written in Pigeonese. A difficult language, but I can usually figure it out." Oliver's nose twitched, as he studied gray globs in the sand. "These are Stool Pigeon droppings."

Oliver handed me a paper and pencil stub from his pocket. "Here. Copy the clues on this piece of paper. Leave the stone, so the Stool Pigeons won't know we're on to them. We'll get a fresh start in the morning."

I scribbled the information, squinting to see in the dimming light. "It sure gets dark fast." Tomorrow would be day two of my time in Drainovia. We had to find the crown soon. Surely, the clues would help.

I followed Oliver and curled up beside him on the sandy floor inside a cave. The pillows and extra clothing warmed and cushioned me, while a soft lemony breeze blew around us. Waves lapping gently at the edge of the beach lulled me to sleep.

Dreams of Captain Scarlet chasing me and putting me in prison haunted me. "But I can't stay here!" I yelled over and over.

Hot sand hit me in the face.

I sputtered and sat up, blinking in the light.

CHAPTER 7

THE sun shone brightly and a fist-sized, beady-eyed hermit crab stared at me, opening and closing his pincers. He looked like he was getting ready to make a stab at me for breakfast.

My stomach growled, almost as loud as the waves crashing on the shore a few yards away.

"Who are ye and what're ye doin' here?" the crab asked in a gravelly voice.

"Herman Hunstable, you old salt. Good to see you." Oliver stretched and rubbed his eyes. Then he scampered up my big pillow. "I thought you'd be at the Crabbenda Convention. Aren't you the outgoing President?"

"Oliver, that 'twas last year. Things have changed, since I stepped down. Ye've not heard then about Roscoe Crabbins?" Herman blinked his eyes and rubbed his pincer in the sand. "Ah, warm sand feels so good. Mornings are rough on me arthritis. Cain't seem to get things moving smoothly anymore."

"Who's Roscoe Crabbins?" I asked, as Oliver climbed into my lap.

"Aargh! He's one o' the Crabbins with old ties to Plumberia. He and his followers have gotten control o' Crabbenda. A pair o' Stool Pigeons acts as his advisors. Rumor has it, they stole Drainovia's crown. As a neutral country, Crabbenda's crabs ain't happy. They even want me to run agin fer President." Herman tossed some warm sand up on his shell. "Hmm. Nothin' like a little sand to freshen up the house."

"What brings you to Drainovia?" Oliver asked.

"I've come to dig up dirt on the Stool Pigeons. If I can prove they be up to no good, then Roscoe'll be forced to resign and all o' Crabbenda will be happy."

"We should join forces. David wants to find Drainovia's crown, so he can get back his mother's ring." Oliver poked me with his paw. "Tell Herman what happened."

I explained about losing my mother's ring. "It seems that the Stool Pigeons took the crown. We found a stone with a map and message in Pigeonese." I showed him the paper.

He squinted. "Let me get me glasses, matey." Reaching into his shell, he pulled out a tiny pair of glasses. "Yes, I see what ye mean. Hmm. 'Where Halibut can be found'. There are lots of places for that. I'll bet Grandpappy might be able to help you narrow it down."

Oliver jumped up, twitching his tail. "Why don't we take the stone and go back with you to Crabbenda? You can show the stone as proof of the Stool Pigeons' involvement with the missing Drainovian Crown. That can't be good for them."

"We can talk to your grandpappy, too." I struggled to my feet, plumped my pillow under my vest, and straightened my tail. I put my hat and Oliver on my head, and then ducked to walk out of the cave. Picking up the stone, I tucked it in the back pocket of my pants and buttoned the pocket.

"Ye look mighty odd in that outfit. Thought ye were a new breed o' drainosaur, when I first saw ye." Herman scuttled behind me. "Wait. Let me hitch a ride on ye."

I stooped to pick him up. "You can ride in one of my vest pockets. They're huge, but handy. Can we use the hat to transport us to Crabbenda, Oliver?"

Oliver released his hold on my hair and peeked out from under the hat. "It won't work between countries without a special add-on device that your hat doesn't have. Once we get there, I'll adjust the harmonics with a simple command. Then we'll be all set to travel within Crabbenda, if you want. It's not very big though."

Herman tapped me with his pincer. "Just follow the beach, and before ye know it we'll be there."

I smelled lemons and spotted a lemon tree on the top of the bank by the water's edge. "I'm hungry. Let me grab a few lemons." Climbing up the bank, I reached the nearest branch to pick a couple pieces of fruit. I put one in another pocket and peeled a big fat lemon. I dropped the peels onto the sand, as I climbed back down.

"These taste good, not tart like the ones at home. Oliver, want a piece?" I held up a section to Oliver.

Oliver sniffed and took a few bites.

"Herman?" I asked.

Herman waved it away with his pincer. "None fer me, matey, I have some leftovers in me shell from last night's dinner. Excuse me while I go in to break me fast." He tucked his body into his shell deep within my pocket.

Finishing the lemon, I kicked sand over the peels. "Don't want Captain Scarlet to know we were here and follow us." I wiped my hands on my pants. "Ready, Oliver, Herman?"

"Yep," Oliver and Herman called.

I began walking. Time passed, as the sun's rays moved overhead and sparkled off the water. Waves slid over the rocks near my feet.

Bees buzzed in a patch of daisies, and a bird cooed in a tree.

Oliver pulled my hair. "Stop!"

CHAPTER 8

I froze.

The cooing continued. An answering coo came from ahead of us.

"That's Pigeonese," Oliver whispered, lifting up the hat to look around us. "Listen."

The cooing stopped.

I stood still, straining to hear. "What did they say?"

"Something about being careful of scarlet roses' sharp thorns." Oliver tapped my head. "Hmm. There's the scarlet rose again. Wonder what it means?"

Herman popped his head out of his shell. "Do ye think they suspect we have their clue?" He swiveled his beady eyes around. "Aargh, I don't see 'em. Those Stool Pigeons use scare tactics, like swooping down at us. Makes a crab feel like they're ready to pluck me right out o' my shell. Nasty birds. I be glad I'm safe in yer pocket. Don't know what Roscoe sees in 'em." Herman pointed his pincer. "Crabbenda is just around the curve in the beach."

I walked along, spotting a few fish swimming through the water. Were they halibut? Around the curve, the beach widened onto a large sandy area. Rocks were piled near a group of trees at the edge of the water.

"Ah, Crabbenda," Herman said. "Set me down and follow closely. Watch yer step."

I put him down and walked behind carefully.

Tiny puffs of sand squirted out around me. A dozen crabs of all sizes appeared. They scurried out of our way, calling to Herman.

"How was yer trip?"

"Who are the strangers?"

"They're friends," Herman replied, as he waved his pincer.

By the time we reached the rocks, dozens of hermit crabs followed. At the top, crawled out a large old crab.

Herman climbed up to join him. "Grandpappy Hunstable, I've brought friends and some news." He turned, pointed his pincer at me, and made the introductions. "Show him what ye've got, David."

I stood beside a lemon tree. Oliver slid to the ground, as I reached to unbutton the back pocket of my pants. I pulled out the stone and set it next to Grandpappy. "We found this back along the beach in Drainovia. Oliver said it was in Pigeonese. It has clues about Drainovia's crown. We think the Stool Pigeons left it for one of their partners in crime."

The old crab slowly rubbed the tip of his pincer along the stone, as he read the message in a deep gravelly voice. "Hmm. The scribbles look the same as the handwriting of the new regulations the Stool Pigeons have been writing fer Roscoe. This could be just what we need to convince the council to ask fer Roscoe's resignation. We cain't have a president who has crooks as his advisors. Ah, thank ye fer helping us." He swiveled his gaze to me. "Why are ye interested in Drainovia's crown?"

"Princess Doris has my mother's ring, that I dropped down our drain. She thinks it's the crown of Drainovia. I thought if I found the real crown, she would give me the ring so I could return home. I've got only today and tomorrow left to find it and get back home." I frowned at the thought.

Grandpappy shook his head. "Aargh. Not an easy task. I fear that if ye are stuck here, yer family's memories about ye may be erased. Strange, but that's the way o' it. Let me think how we can help ye." Grandpappy looked across the salty sea to a distant mountain. "Halibut used to be plentiful from Crabbenda all the way to Plumberia. Now there are only a few spots. Pretty tricky to reach, too."

He scratched a map on a nearby rock. "At the base o' Rose Mountain is a big wide harbor full o' halibut. The Plumberians fish there all the time. This spot here." He scratched an X. "And this one here." He scratched another X. "Both are between Crabbenda and Plumberia. They have plenty o' halibut. Not much sand, but lots o' reeds and kinda marshy. Make sure to avoid those Marsh Fellows at the first X and the trolls in Trollsylvania here at the second X. Be very careful."

I swallowed. This was going to be a lot harder than I thought. "Who or what are the Marsh Fellows?"

"They're a family of giant frogs," said Grandpappy. "They try to catch us. Always yapping 'bout one thing or another."

"Yeah, those Marsh Fellows be a scary, slimy bunch," said one of the crabs beside me. He shuddered and tossed a pincer of sand over his shoulder.

"They have a strange weakness ye might be able to use to get by them." Grandpappy reached into his crusty shell and pulled out a claw full of small dried beans. "They love to eat pinto beans. I find 'em tasty, too. Give me gas, but I like to raise a stink now and then." He laughed, smacking his pincer on the rocks.

Oliver giggled. "I've been known to make a stink about a few things myself." He twirled his tail.

"Thanks." Chuckling, I dropped the beans into my vest pocket. "Ah, what about the trolls? Are they real?" I shuddered, thinking about trolls from fairytales Mama used to read to me.

"Yep, big nasty, ugly brutes. Dumb, but ye don't want them to catch ye. Don't need to add to their diet, if ye know what I mean. If ye stay under cover of the plumberry bushes, ye can avoid them." Grandpappy coughed, as several crabs tossed more pincers of sand.

Oliver tapped the stone. "What do you think about the scarlet rose? How does that fit in?"

Grandpappy shrugged. "I think the Plumberian King Thomas' last name is Rose. Other than that, I don't recall any scarlet roses around here."

One of the other old crusty crabs coughed. "I seem to remember a patch of thorny roses at the base of Rose Mountain. Ain't that how they got their name? Ain't a rose part of their royal crest?" He scratched his shell. "Don't know if it's a scarlet one, though."

"Yes, Grandpappy. That old book you found told us about the Plumberians," said a smaller crab.

"Yep, yer right. Dig under this pile of stones for me Herman. It be near the bottom. David, make yerself at home 'til he gets the book." The crusty crab coughed again. Most of the rest of the crabs returned to their places in the sand.

Grandpappy used his pincer to drag the stone with the pigeons' message under a bigger pile of rocks. "This'll keep it safe 'til the council can meet tomorrow."

I was hungry. "Hey Oliver, why don't you catch a couple of fish for our lunch?" I started gathering a pile of sticks and dried brush.

"There's plenty more sticks." Grandpappy scuttled ahead of me to where grass poked out from the sand. Twigs and loose branches from a nearby tree lay there.

Oliver looked at me, paws on his hips. "You start the fire, and I'll have a couple fish in no time." He splashed about in the water.

Packing some dried grass and small twigs into a pile, I held my magnifying glass over the pile to catch the rays of the sun.

Poof! Smoke curled up from the twigs and grass. I fed more sticks into the growing fire. Oliver, splashing about in the water, tossed two small fish at me.

"No! Please, don't eat us!" The fish flopped around, trying to get back into the water.

Oh, you've got to be kidding!

I let the fish go back into the water. "I guess it's lemons again."

Soft waves washed the shore, as a slight breeze blew through my hair. I sat on one of my pillows beside Grandpappy's rock pile and put my hat and the big fat pillow next to me.

"Well, mateys, I found the book," said Herman. He dragged it over near the fire.

I reached for it. "Thanks." The cover was decorated with a coat of arms that showed a rose twisted around a fish. Maybe it would help me understand what I was up against. I opened the book. "It's in a strange language." It reminded me of the Pig Latin my friend Tim's mother and father used when they didn't want us to know what they were talking about. We figured it out though. "Hmm. It divides the words and puts the first consonant sound at the end with the sound 'umb' with it. 'Umberia-plumb Oyal-rumb Egistry-rumb' must be Plumberia Royal Registry."

"The 'b' sound in Plumberia is silent." Grandpappy rubbed his pincer in the warm sand. "But they talk more like ye do now."

Oliver turned the page. "Look. Here's a picture of the royal family that founded the country."

"They're people like me!" I exclaimed.

CHAPTER 9

OLIVER twitched his tail. "Yes, but you don't look exactly like them. You have dark hair and darker skin than they do. Every one of them has yellow hair and pale skin."

Grandpappy peered at the page, and then looked up at me. "I believe ye be taller than a lot o' the Plumberians."

I looked closer at the book. "Tell me about them."

"A hundred years ago, they came to Drainovia," said Grandpappy. "My great-grandpappy told me that they didn't see eye to eye with the Drainovian King, so they left to start their own kingdom. One of the King's Royal Advisors took the Royal Building Code secrets and left with 'em. They've been enemies ever since."

Herman swatted a fly with his pincer. "Yep, the last war was over Drain Rights. The Drainovians have upper rights and that left the lower rights to the Plumberians. They wanted passage to the upper drains, too. Drainovia refused. At the war's end, the Drainovian Crown was stolen, and the Plumberian Prince had disappeared."

Grandpappy scratched his shell. "Guess their problems at home were gettin' so bad, they had to sign a peace agreement. They made peace, but both kingdoms lost heart and blame the other fer their problems. Not sure how long the peace will last."

"Wow. We have wars where I come from, too." I turned some pages.

"Shame we all cain't get along." Grandpappy shook his head.

"Look!" I pointed to another page. "Here's a list of family names and cities. This one says: 'Lord Wilber and Lady Scarlet Rose, 615 Scarlet Lane, Plungerville'. They must be related to King Thomas."

"Yep. That's where the palace is now." Herman tapped his pincer against his shell. "My cousin delivers a load o' sand twice a year to his friend in Plungerville. He's supposed to go again soon, I think."

"What does 'a case is closed on a scarlet rose' mean, now?" I scratched my head.

Grandpappy turned a few more pages. "Cain't be talkin' 'bout Scarlet Rose. She'd be dead by now. This is old. Must be a lot more people in Plumberia, since this was written."

"How did they get here?" I sat and buried the lemon peels in the sand.

"Long ago it was said there was a great earthquake topside and quite a few families landed in Drainovia." Herman squinted at the book and then pushed up his glasses. "Hmm. It says: 'After the Falling due to the Great Earthquake of 1906, the land of the mountains became our home. Connections to the past were lost and a new life was forged on this great frontier. Relations with the neighboring creatures of the Kingdom called Drainovia were strained and an Old One, an advisor in Drainovia took pity and came with us. We are indebted to her valuable scientific knowledge and dedicate the town of Plungerville to her. Long live Plumberia!'"

I leaned over the book. "Whoa. 'Falling' must mean they fell into drains or a sewer or something. There are lots of earthquakes in some parts of my country, like in California, and small ones even where I live."

Oliver clapped his paws. "There you have it. The Roses must've been important people that fell down here and started their own country."

"Why didn't they just use a hat and go home?" I asked.

"Hats are a fairly recent invention in Drainovia. I'm surprised Princess Doris told you about them." Oliver patted the hat. "She must've wanted you to go home pretty badly."

I nodded. "Yeah, she probably realized that what she thought was the crown was my mother's ring after all. I'm surprised she's not still looking for the real crown. Maybe that's why it was so easy to escape from the tower. Could she think I'd lead her to the real crown?"

"Princess Doris is stubborn," said Herman. "If she said it was the real crown, it would take a team o' wild doors threatening to carry her to Plumberia to change her mind. 'Course if she wasn't sure, she might be watchin' ye. Have ye been followed?"

I shook my head. "I don't think so. We've been covering our tracks."

I remembered the door that I'd ridden into Drainovia. "They have a lot of strange technology in use down here. We don't have flying doors or teleporting hats."

"Maybe it's the lemons. They really sharpen the intellect." Oliver scampered up a low tree limb and tossed a lemon to me.

I laughed as I caught it. "Then I better eat a lot to figure out what we should do next."

"Pack yer pockets full," Grandpappy suggested. "They'll satisfy yer thirst, too."

"Thanks. I guess I will. These lemons are sweeter than the ones we have at home. Those will really pucker your lips." I loaded my pockets with the fruit, thinking back to last weekend, when my little brother had tried to sell lemonade and how I ended up buying most of it after I cut the grass. He'd love these lemons. I picked up my hat.

Oliver jumped out of the tree and onto my head. Climbing part way under the hat, he tapped my forehead. "Don't forget the rest of your costume. We're still close to Drainovia so you'll need it. Hurry. I don't want to get caught by the Marsh Fellows or the trolls."

"Right. Thanks, everyone!" I tucked one pillow into my pants and vest, and then pinned on my tail pillow. "I hope you get Roscoe to resign. What will you do about the Stool Pigeons? Won't they think you're after the Drainovian crown?"

"They don't think we're very smart. Roscoe's trusted them to run practically everything." Grandpappy laughed. "Won't they be surprised?"

"Do you think they'll move the crown?" I asked.

Herman shook his head. "We'll be watching them, so I don't think they would try. They'll probably be chirping about how innocent they are."

Oliver waved. "Goodbye. We'll see you on our way back."

With a wave, I started walking down the beach, following the map that Grandpappy had drawn on the stone. Several boats bobbed across the sea. "What are they doing?"

"Hmm, could be just fishing for halibut," said Oliver. "They're the only fish that don't talk. We'll have to keep an eye on them." He yawned. "Wake me up when we get near the first X."

"Fine. If I have to use the hat, I just think of where I need to go, right?"

"Yeah, we're out of Crabbenda and back in Drainovia." Oliver's muffled voice grew quiet. His soft snoring sounded almost like a purr.

Eating lemons, I walked along. I kicked a shell. Oops, Mama would've liked that pink one. I bent to pick it up. I'd give it to her when I got home, if I got back in time. My lips trembled, as I rubbed a hand across my eyes. Taking a deep breath, I stood and straightened my shoulders. I had to get her ring back and go home. I just had to!

The sun's rays reflected off the water, making me squint. I barely noticed when the beach narrowed and reeds grew close to the water's edge. Still thinking of home, I bent down to pick up a wide, flat stone to skip across the water.

"Drop it," a voice croaked.

CHAPTER 10

I stood straight and found a frog sitting beside me. It was bigger than I was. His eyes bulged, and his tongue flicked out, catching a fly. Water glistened on his bluish-green skin that pulsed and jiggled as he moved.

Startled, I turned and tripped on my tail pillow. My hat slid off onto the sand, dumping out Oliver.

"Hey!" Oliver sat up.

The frog blinked, and then pointed at the stones. "They look like skippers, but they're sinkers fer sure. Don't waste yer time. Why are ya here? We don't get many visitors. Come meet my family."

A frog leg wrapped around me and tugged me through the reeds into the water. Another frog hopped over to Oliver. He scooted after me, stopping at the edge of the water.

A couple of large frogs sat on huge lily pads.

Slowed down by my wet pillows, I sloshed over to them.

The largest frog pointed at my pillows. "Are you Drainosaur or Plumberian? Why are you dressed like that?"

"Since I'm in Drainovia, I need to look more like them to blend in." I struggled to keep my balance, as my feet sank in the mud.

Another large frog waggled a finger. "George, he's shivering. Take him back to shore, so he can get out of those wet things. Don't want our guests to catch cold."

George and I struggled toward the sand. As the frog let me go, I reached for the reeds. Oliver squirmed in the grasp of a smaller frog, a female I guessed by the strands of flowers looped around her neck.

"Look, Mommy! I found a cute one. Can he stay for dinner?" The smaller frog petted Oliver's head, and her long tongue darted out to kiss him.

"Aaagh." Oliver dug his paws into the frog's hand.

"Oh, Mommy!" The frog dropped Oliver and hopped up and down, waving her sore hand.

Oliver ran and jumped onto my shoulder.

"Children! You cannot force friends to join us. Be nice."

Water splashed, as the four frogs hopped to the sand and circled around Oliver and me.

"They will stay with us, right?" The biggest frog leaned over me. His watery eyes were almost as big as my head.

"Yes," I squeaked, jerking backwards to avoid his drippy eyes.

"Take off those wet things. I will fix some food." The mother frog turned to the reeds. She pulled out a bag that wiggled. "Hope you like big juicy bugs. They are tasty and our favorite."

"Um, I have some delicious beans you can have, too." I handed the pinto beans to her.

"Great! How nice. I will fix them quickly." She hopped away.

The biggest frog poked my waterlogged pillows. "I help you."

"Uh, that's okay. I can do it myself." Water dripping, I unpinned and took them off. I squeezed out the water and set them to dry in the sun. Hanging the clothes on nearby tree branches, I hoped they would dry quickly. My shoes and socks were wet, but I didn't dare remove them.

"Your hair is so dark. Is it natural?" The smallest frog blinked her eyes and touched me with a long thin finger.

I batted away her hand. "Of course, it is."

Two other frogs joined the group. One laughed, as it tried on my hat.

"Look! It's the latest fashion." The frog hopped up and down as another frog snatched at it.

"I want a hat like that, Papa." The smallest frog pulled on her father's leg. "Please, Papa?"

I grabbed the hat. "It's not the latest fashion. Just keeps my head cool from all the sun." I put on the hat and looked for Oliver.

"Bug Bean Delight is ready!" the mother frog yelled. "Let's eat."

The frogs turned, hopping toward her.

Oliver and I had to get away from these Marsh Fellows. I was not going to eat bugs for dinner. The frogs were huge and there was no telling how big 'supper' would be. *Ugh!* From the looks of the bag that the mother frog had held, the bugs were still alive.

Oliver jumped on my shoulders and climbed under my hat. I ran, grabbing my wet pillows and clothes.

The amazed faces of the frogs blurred and swirled, as Oliver and I disappeared.

CHAPTER 11

WE reappeared on a wide sandy stretch of beach, that rose to a cliff in the distance. A slight wind rustled the leaves in a few crooked trees nearby. At least this time I didn't feel sick from the teleporting.

"Where are we, Oliver?" I dropped the now dry pillows, vest, and pants on the sand. Teleporting had wrung out the water from everything.

"I think we're just down the beach a little from those Marsh Fellows. Good thing you gave them some beans, so they won't be mad at us. I'll bet there are some interesting caves around here. We'll have to be on the lookout." Oliver slid to the ground and walked along the beach.

I put on my costume and followed, studying Grandpappy's map. "We're not too far from the first X. See that big dead tree over there? He said Halibut could be found there."

Oliver smacked his lips. "Great! We can eat halibut for supper."

"You can catch one, while I look for a place that could hide a crown. That old tree might be a great hiding place." I walked toward the tree.

Large, gnarly branches twisted all around a thick trunk full of mottled bark. In a notch of a lower limb, I saw a dark patch of bark with a row of scratches that looked like Pigeonese. I touched an edge of the bark. It moved and came off, revealing a hole in the tree. A sparkling pale-yellow stone reflected the sunlight. I reached in and pulled it out. "Hey, Oliver! I found a diamond just like the ones in Mama's ring!" I replaced the bark to cover the hole.

Oliver trotted over, dragging a large flopping fish. "I've got our supper. Let's see this diamond."

I sat on the ground to hold it out to him.

He dropped the fish. "Wow, sure is pretty. If it looks like your mama's, do you think it's part of the crown?" Oliver peered at the stone. Then scratched his head. "Why would they take the diamonds out of it?"

"I don't have a clue." I turned it over in my hand. "I better keep this in my jeans pocket. We don't want to lose it. Do you think they took out all three diamonds?" I tucked it inside.

"I don't know." Oliver shrugged. "If so, maybe they hid them nearby."

"Take a look at the scratches on the tree. It looks like Pigeonese." I walked over to the tree and pointed. "See? Right there by that notch."

Oliver jumped on the low branch to study the marks. "Yeah, it says 'the worms may feed on berry seed at' and then I can't read it. There's just a bunch of uneven cuts."

"Are there worms around here?"

"Here, no. I only know of one kind of worm that eats berry seeds. They lived far underground. No one has seen one in years." Oliver ran down the tree and back to the fish. "Let's eat!"

"Wait a minute. What kind of worm are you talking about?"

Oliver tugged at the fish. "It's not really a worm. It's called the Psychedelic Caterpillar. It has two heads with big purple, orange, and green stripes."

I picked up the fish and rinsed it in the water. "I'll clean this, while you gather sticks for a fire. So where does this worm live?"

"I'm not sure. I think it might live near Trollsylvania." Oliver dumped a pile of twigs at my feet.

Soon a fire blazed, and the fish cooked on sticks above it. I added more driftwood from under the tree to stoke the fire.

"Smells great." Oliver licked his lips.

"Here you go. Enjoy." I handed him some fish. Pulling a piece off my stick, I popped it into my mouth and chewed. "I guess we should head toward Plumberia. We'll go to the next place Grandpappy marked on his map on the way. Maybe we'll find the crown or another diamond."

Oliver patted his stomach, burped, and then stretched. "Come to think of it, the only reason they would take the diamonds out of the crown was if they had power. Remember I told you about the link to prosperity? If the diamonds are separated, perhaps their power is weakened. Nobody would have all the power in their hands, if they found the crown minus a gemstone or two."

"But why wouldn't someone who stole the crown want to keep all of the stones together?" I finished eating, and then piled sand over the logs to put out the fire.

Oliver took a stick to poke at a piece of fish stuck in his teeth, and then spat. "Maybe the Stool Pigeons stole the crown, but didn't completely trust whoever they were stealing it for."

"Then why steal it?" I shook sand from my hands and stood.

Oliver shrugged and started walking.

I trailed after Oliver, gazing at our surroundings. The beach sloped up, forming a cliff. In parts, it hung high over the sand. Grass waved in the breeze along the top. Rocks lay scattered down below. Much farther ahead

I could see patches of bushes jutting out from the cliff.

Oliver's overalls snagged on some branches, pulling him to a stop. "Hey, there's a cave hidden behind these bushes. I've never seen this one before. You better stay here while I check this out." He untangled himself, and then darted inside the cave.

I listened to the waves break on the shore. They were getting louder, and a fine salty mist sprayed the nearby rocks. The boats that I had seen earlier were no longer out on the water. The sun cast long shadows as it sat on top of the mountain.

"David, come look at this!"

I squished my pillows and squeezed through the narrow opening. It widened into a large vault. The little bit of light that came in sparkled off a large white pillar in the center.

When I touched the pillar, the smooth cool surface reflected my finger. As I looked closer, the column became more transparent. "Wow, this is amazing!"

Suddenly an old woman's face appeared in the pillar. Her mouth moved and her head shook.

Startled, I jerked my hand away.

"David, come over here quick!" Ahead, Oliver stood beside a wooden door.

I hurried to him. Sand, small pebbles, and dry leaves had blown inside, piling up at the bottom of the door. The hinges were corroded, and a padlock hung from a rusted latch.

"What is a door doing here?" I spotted a ledge carved in the wall beside the door. Above Oliver, I could see some faint writing on the door. "This looks like the same writing that was in the book that Grandpappy found. It's Plumberian. It says: 'Elper-humb of an-mumb ives-lumb ere-humb.' Helper of man lives here." I scratched my head.

"That's weird," Oliver said. "I heard lots of stories about Plumberians when I was little, but nothing about this place." Oliver started to dig into the sand at the base of the door.

"That's not the only thing weird here. Check out the face." I pointed to the pillar.

"What face?"

I led him to the pillar. "Watch." I held out a finger. An inner light flashed and the pillar grew crystal clear.

The old woman's face appeared. "What are the crossing words?" she asked in a soft voice.

"Wow!" Oliver jumped back.

"Crossing words?" I looked down at Oliver. "What could it be?"

Oliver scratched his head. "Hmm. Rose? Scarlet? Wilber?"

I repeated the words, but each time the old woman shook her head.

"You may not cross. Leave this place at once." The woman's face in the pillar faded and disappeared. Once again, the pillar was opaque.

I dropped my hand. "Okay, that didn't work. What do you think we should do now?"

"This place is well hidden, so why don't we stay the night? We can even dig out the door." Oliver twitched his tail, as he looked around the cave. He scooted over to the door to scoop up pawfuls of sand that he tossed to the side.

As much as I hated to lose time from our search on day two, I knew he was right. If we got a really early start, hopefully we could find the rest of the diamonds and the crown in the morning. Then I'd return to Drainovia for Mama's ring.

I sighed. "I'll get dry twigs and start a fire."

I took off my pillows and hat and set them on the ledge. At the entrance I broke off dry dead branches from the bushes and set them inside in a pile. I walked outside, closer to the water to pick up two pieces of dry driftwood. The air was cooler, but there was just enough sun to magnify onto the wood for a fire. I carried the lit pieces carefully into the cave. I gathered more wood, added some to the fire, and set aside the rest to use through the night.

Every now and then I glanced at the pillar trying to think of the password.

"Whew, this is hard work!" Oliver dumped a pawful of sand, and then wiped sandy paws on his overalls. A mound of stones, sand, and leaves lay around him.

"Come take a break. I'm thirsty. Let's eat a couple of lemons. I still have some left in my pocket." I sat down to peel the lemons.

Oliver joined me. He munched on a lemon and smacked his lips. "Ah, this hits the spot."

I laughed. "You remind me of that old room full of drainosaurs sucking all those lemons. Boy, they were noisy." I squirted Oliver in the face as I peeled another lemon.

"Here, I'll open my mouth and you can try that again." Oliver danced around with his mouth open.

I took aim and squirted juice right into his mouth. Oliver gulped and clapped his paws. I handed him part of the lemon. "You can eat this and I'll finish the rest."

After eating, we tossed the peels into the fire. It crackled and spit sparks. I looked at the entrance to the cave and around the big room. The fire cast giant shadows on the wall near the wooden door.

"Do you think anyone will see the fire?" I made rabbit faces with my hands and moved them around to attack Oliver beside the door.

Oliver tumbled backward trying to get away from the shadows on the door. He turned to glare at me. "Cute trick. No, the bushes will shield it. Someone would have to look closely to see there's even a cave here."

"Good. I'll give you a hand." I sat beside him and started digging.

Finally, we brushed away the last grains of sand and studied the door.

"How do we open it?" Oliver scratched his head. "The lock is old, but not as rusty as the hinges."

I examined the lock. "Some rust is scratched away. Someone must have used it a little while ago. It probably doesn't take long for the sand to build up against the door. Look at the fire flicker." I pointed. "See how the wind blows around in here?"

"Yeah." Oliver wiggled his whiskers. "Who do you think was here?"

"Would the Plumberians have used this during the war? Do you think the frogs or the crabs have been here? Could drainosaurs travel this way along the sea?"

Oliver shook his head. "Drainosaurs don't come here, and the frogs are too big to fit inside. If the crabs knew about this, Herman would've told us, especially since it has this door and that talking pillar."

"This is across the sea from the Plumberians, right? What would they do here? Hide from Drainovians?" I ran my hands around the edge of the door.

"Since I don't think the Drainovians know about this cave, the Plumberians could've hid here. What are you doing?"

"In movies they always do this. They look for hidden levers or buttons on panels to open secret passages." Finished, I wiped my dirty hands on my pants. "Wait a minute, this is a long shot but maybe my key will fit the lock. It's an old one that I found the other day." I reached deep into a back pocket and pulled it out. It mostly fit. One turn and a little jiggling of the key opened the lock. Removing it, I lifted the latch and pulled on the door. It creaked open.

Beside me, Oliver grabbed my hat. "Whoa. Here, hold onto your hat, just in case."

I held it in my hand, as Oliver climbed up my vest and into a big pocket.

Suddenly, wind gusted toward us from beyond the door and blew out the fire. I turned back to see just a few embers shedding a faint eerie glow.

"Stop where you are," a shrill voice barked. "You cannot enter."

I spun around, dropping my hat.

Through the doorway there was only darkness. Then four small pinpoints of light winked at me.

CHAPTER 12

STRAINING to see where the voice had come from, I stepped forward. I held my hands in front of me and touched a warm, pudgy glob.

"Noooo, back we say, back!"

Something swatted at my hands. Hundreds of tiny hairs swept over my body, pulsing in the air around me. I tumbled into a soft glob and fell onto a rough stone floor.

"Ruined! It's all your fault!" The high voice whined.

As my eyes adjusted to the dim light, I saw a large two-headed caterpillar rolling on the floor beside me in the stone passageway. The two heads swiveled wildly and six legs scrambled to stand the creature upright. A cottony mass lay beside it.

I jumped up, trying to get away from the creature. My hands clutched at the rocky walls, and my head touched the ceiling. Cobwebs stuck to my nose and lips.

"*Pbbtt*," I spat, wiping my mouth with the back of my hand. I hoped there weren't any spiders. I hated spiders. Shivering, I wiped my face and peered at the caterpillar.

"We are very heartbroken. How can we make the change without our cocoon? Without it we will die!" Each head moaned and cried. "There is only three of our kind left. We don't want to become extinct!"

"Wow, a real Psychedelic Caterpillar!" Oliver wiggled and clapped his paws, almost falling out of my pocket. "Do you have a name?"

"I am Gert," said one head with rosy pink cheeks.

"And I am Trudy." The second, paler head moaned and cried again.

I shoved Oliver back in place. "He's Oliver and I'm David. I'm sorry about your cocoon, but it was a silly place to put it."

The pink-cheeked Gert looked up at me. "This is our home, so it's not silly to us. You ruined our cocoon. Now we need to get more plumberries to eat to produce the fiber to make our cocoon again."

"Plumberries are tasty, but hard to get. Oh, what a shame!" Trudy moaned, getting even paler. "We need two big baskets of plumberries. It took us days to get the right amount. Soon it will be too hot, and they will be gone." She started crying again making the entire caterpillar's hairs shake on its trembling body.

Gert started to cry, too.

I swallowed. All I wanted was to get to Plumberia, find the Drainovian crown, get my mother's ring and go home. But if it weren't for me, they would be okay. I couldn't let them die. Lowering my head, I sighed. "Wait, don't cry. I'll help you get the berries."

Both heads peered at me. "Really?" They sniffled loudly, and then leaned down to blow their wet noses on part of the cottony mass.

I took a big breath. "Yeah, sure. Tell me where these bushes are and what they look like. Can we go back into the cave and sit by what's left of the fire to talk?"

"Okay, we will talk there." The caterpillar followed me.

Oliver jumped down from my pocket and pulled a piece of wood to the dying embers.

I blew on the embers carefully, as I fed smaller pieces to build up the fire. As it blazed, I sat down on my tail pillow.

The caterpillar stood nearby. Its stripes of bright orange, green, and purple rippled in the firelight as it tapped two of its many little red-slippered feet. Thin silvery hairs fluttered all around its body. Little caps rested on top of each head. The caterpillar must have been as big as my neighbor's pony at home.

"I guess you were ready for bed." I pointed to the slippers and hats.

"Yes," Gert said with sigh. "We almost finished our cocoon and were getting ready to settle in for our long rest. Then you fell and broke the outer shell."

"And we were looking forward to waking up with fine gold-dotted purple wings. What a shame." Trudy shook her head, wiping a tear with a red-slippered foot.

"I'm sorry. Can't you make another cocoon and get your wings?"

"We hope so, if the berries aren't already gone this year. If not, we will die," said Trudy. The caterpillar's body shuddered.

"We're tired of dark tunnels and living underground like we have for the last five years. Oh, to soar high and free for eternity!" Gert wiggled a hairy leg. It shimmered silver. Then it changed to different colors before the firelight, like the fiber-optic Christmas tree we had at home.

"Where exactly are these plumberries?"

"They are on the side of Rose Mountain in Trollsylvania."

"Trollsylvania!" My jaw dropped. I shuddered at the idea of a run in with trolls.

"Yes. Red Hair-Ring is the troll leader. I think he wants to eat all of the Plumberians and rule the Drainosaurs. He's so mean. He eats little Plumberian children for breakfast! He takes their hair first, dips it in blood and makes a huge ugly hair-ring he wears in his nose." All four eyes of the caterpillar blinked tearfully at me.

"So we *have* to go to Trollsylvania?" Oliver frowned at the caterpillar in disbelief.

"Yes, the dense Plumberry bushes form a canopy in Trollsylvania. The trolls love the shade there," said Gert.

"They like to pick on us as we collect berries. The last time, they threatened to eat us!" Trudy began to cry again.

"Please, don't cry!" I said with groan.

Oliver twitched his tail. "How do you know trolls eat Plumberians?"

"Well, I guess we've never really seen them eat a Plumberian. It is just a story we've heard." Gert lifted a leg to rub her chin.

Trudy turned to look at Gert. "Do you think the Plumberian parents just tell that to their children to keep them close to home?"

"Could be." Gert shrugged. "I'll bet they don't want to take any chances."

"If that's true, where did Red Hair-Ring get his rings of hair?" Trudy's eyes widened. "You don't suppose—"

Gert looked at Trudy. "No, that would be too horrible!" The caterpillar's body hairs shimmered red, as it trembled.

CHAPTER 13

"YOU said he was called Red Hair-Ring?"

I fed another small stick to the fire. Sparks shot out swirling up past the scared faces of the caterpillar as they nodded. The tiny hairs on their body still shimmered blood red. I blinked and swallowed. Red Hair-Ring might not eat little Plumberian children, but he might eat caterpillars. I wondered if there were just three Psychedelic Caterpillars alive.

I stoked the fire. "Are there many trolls? What are their names?"

"We saw a few lurking in trees near the trail," said Gert.

"Yes, but none as big as Red Hair-Ring. I heard him talk to one he called Blister." Trudy made a face at the name. "Yuck!"

"Did you get a good look at him?" I asked.

"He didn't have a hair-ring but he was hairy and had big bumps all over him."

"He was the one that kept scratching his back on that oak tree. He chewed on some leaves, too. He spat right at me." Trudy wrinkled her nose. "Good thing we were hidden in the bushes and covered with mud."

"Yes, they don't see very well, but they can smell a stranger from far away unless their natural odor is camouflaged." Gert giggled. "You looked so funny, Trudy." Gert shook with laughter. "All you could see was her big white eyes in a brown muddy mess."

"Well, you looked just as funny." Trudy sniffed.

"But I didn't eat the mud. I told you it was stinky and buggy. You looked so funny when you licked your lips covered with those little ladybugs. I almost gave away our position trying not to laugh at you." Gert chortled, almost rolling the whole caterpillar onto the floor of the cave.

"Humph!" Trudy struggled upright. "Good thing Red Hair-Ring didn't see us. That would've been your last laugh."

Gert's face grew serious. "Yours, too."

"When we go to these Plumberry bushes, we'll have to be covered in mud. Where do we do this?" Oliver warmed his paws by the fire.

"At the base of Rose Mountain in the puddles by the bushes."

I stretched my arms over my head. "I guess we'll have a long walk to get there."

"No, not really." Gert pointed to the pillar. "We can use the Pillar of Lady Scarlet or just go through the passage where you found us."

"The woman in the pillar is Lady Scarlet? You mean Lord Wilber's wife? That's weird." Oliver looked at me. "Do you realize that Captain Scarlet has the same name?" He twitched his tail at the pillar in the middle of the room.

Trudy and Gert waddled over to the column. "Lady Scarlet was Lord Wilbur's wife. She recorded an interactive visual-gram long ago to help Plumberian travelers. You're not a Plumberian, so how do you know about her? And who is Captain Scarlet?"

"Captain Scarlet is head of the Drainovian Police and Armed Forces. He couldn't be related to her. That is odd, though. Grandpappy Hunstable had a book about the Plumberians." I joined them at the pillar. "When I touched this, she asked for the crossing words. I have no clue what that means. Do you?"

"It depends on where you want to go. You just say the name of the place, how many are going, how long you want to stay. Then it zaps you there." Trudy touched the pillar with a red-slippered foot.

The pillar began to glow and pulse. Lady Scarlet appeared. "What are the crossing words?"

Gert waved a foot at Oliver and me. "Better get over here."

I dumped sand on the fire, until only a few embers glowed.

We crowded around the pillar.

Trudy leaned close to Lady Scarlet. "The Plumberry bushes in Trollsylvania. Three for a two-hour round trip."

"Take your places and return to the sending spot in two hours."

Lights swirled in the room like the light off a mirrored ball on a Christmas tree. The next thing I knew, I was flying through the air in the dark. I tumbled through wet leaves and branches to the ground. Oliver landed next to me. A gust of wood smoke came from nearby. The bright moon peeked out from behind the clouds.

A red-slippered foot tapped my shoulder. "Quick. Over here."

I followed the caterpillar under the branches of a tree and slid into a huge mud puddle. "Gross!"

"Smear it all over. Remember not to eat it," Trudy whispered.

As if I would be tempted to eat this stinking mess, I thought, rubbing it on my clothes and skin.

Oliver, covered from head to toe in the mud, wiggled his whiskers, sending a crawly bug into the air to land on one of Gert's feet.

She kicked her foot and fell into the mud. Trudy rolled her eyes, struggling to stand.

"Let's hide in the Plumberry bushes and start filling this basket." Gert pointed to a basket hidden under a bush. It was as big as the caterpillar.

"Do we need to fill two of *that*?" I asked. How did she expect me to find berries in the dark, when I could barely see in front of me? Hopefully the moonlight would help, once my eyes adjusted from being in front of the bright fire in the cave.

"We fill it in two hours. Take it back. Dump it. Then return. It should be a lot easier, since you and Oliver are here to help. It took us twice as long by ourselves. This way, we'll be faster and less likely to have the trolls catch us." Gert shuddered as she took off her slippers and set them inside the basket. Trudy followed. They sat and used all six feet to pick berries. For every six picked, they tossed a couple into their mouths. Purple berry goo dripped off their muddy chins.

Oliver and I sat under another bush, picked and tossed berries into the basket. I tasted a berry. It was tart and sweet at the same time. I popped in a few more, and thought they would make a great pie. Oliver wiped his mouth with a paw. Berry juice stained his dirty whiskers.

"Hey," I whispered. "We'd better fill the basket instead of our stomachs."

As the pile of berries in the basket grew, I wondered about the trolls. So far, we hadn't seen or heard them. Maybe the mud really did protect us from being detected.

"That should do it." Gert and Trudy pushed up onto their purple-stained feet.

Oliver and I wiped berry juice from his paws and my hands. "How do we get back?"

"We stand under the tree over there by the mud puddle and wait. It shouldn't be long." The caterpillar wiggled over to it.

I dragged the basket under the tree. We stood and waited. Light flashed and soon we were tumbling onto the floor of the cave. The basket of berries spilled a little as it landed.

"Whew! You stink!" Oliver rubbed a paw over his nose, flaking off some mud.

"Yeah, well you don't smell like roses, either." I turned to Gert. "Where do you want the plumberries?"

"Back in our passageway beside the old cocoon. We can try to reuse part of the broken cocoon for our bed in the new one."

Oliver and I pushed the basket into the passageway where Gert and Trudy turned it over.

"Do you think one more trip will do it?" I asked.

"Oh yes, it should give us enough." Trudy and Gert popped a couple berries into their mouths as they walked back to the pillar. "Ready?"

"Let's go."

In no time we were back in Trollsylvania, picking plumberries to fill the basket. As the berries neared the top, the ground rumbled and shook.

"Oh no! The trolls are coming! Hide deep in the mud." Gert and Trudy pushed the basket ahead into the puddle. They rolled down into the mud, dragging the basket with them. Only their faces and the berries shown.

Oliver and I dove in trying to hide in the mud. My head, arms, and legs still stuck out. Oliver was beside Gert who pushed him under.

"Ah, what we have here?" A strong hairy arm grabbed my legs, yanked me out and threw me to the ground.

CHAPTER 14

FEAR knotted my stomach, as I gasped for breath.

A large troll with a red hair ring hanging from his nose leaned down. I gagged at the smell of rotten meat that came from his open, laughing mouth.

"You aren't Plumberian or Drainovian, so who are you?" The troll picked a bug off his nose and ate it. Dark, bloodshot eyes glared at me by the light of the torch he carried.

"I'm David," I stammered, scrambling backward.

"David, you will come with me." He swatted a big hand at me. I tumbled further away from the mud puddle. He grabbed my shirt and pulled me to my feet. "Let's hear your story, before we eat you." He laughed.

I gagged again.

He dragged me through the trees into a clearing. In the middle, a bonfire crackled sending sparks into the moonlit sky. A group of trolls sat roasting big hunks of food on sticks over the fire. I didn't want to know what they were eating. I just hoped I wouldn't end up on a stick.

"What you bring us?" A large lumpy looking troll lumbered over to us.

Red Hair-Ring pushed me near the fire. "A stranger."

"Maybe he tastes good." The lumpy troll prodded me with his stick.

Red Hair-Ring grabbed the stick and broke it. "Stop, Blister. He looks different and is bigger. This one can talk and tell us new stories first. Then we eat him." The troll grinned and licked his lips.

"Sit. Talk of where you come from."

In the distance I saw a flash of light. The caterpillar and Oliver were probably returning to the cave. Hopefully they had enough plumberries. At least they were safe. I wished Oliver had stayed to help me, but what could a little ferret do? Besides, I knew he should return to his family. Too bad I didn't have my teleporting hat.

A finger jabbed me in the ribs. "Talk or we eat you now."

I glanced around at the big ugly brutes as I sat down and told the story of The Three Little Pigs. "And the wolf came down the chimney and the pigs caught him in a big pot of water and boiled him up."

"Smart little pigs. Wolf taste good?" Blister drooled, eyeing me as if I was one.

Red Hair-Ring stretched out beside the fire. "Tell another story."

I told the story of Little Red Riding Hood.

"Granny not taste good. Old meat tough! Now tell about your home. You come from Plumberia or Drainovia?" Red Hair-Ring pushed a large log on the fire. It crackled and a burst of sparks flew into the sky.

"Ah, I live in a land far beyond the mountains." I described my home and added details about an imaginary land where dragons breathed fire and trolls were slaves, until they were freed by a mighty warrior king. "Then King Fearless killed the last dragon. He freed Princess Debra, whom he married. All the trolls worked hard to prepare a feast to celebrate. They decided the King was brave and the beautiful Princess fair and worthy of their devotion. So they all lived happily ever after."

Snores filled the night air. Red Hair-Ring slept with one beefy hand around my foot. Blister and the other trolls snored, stretched out beside the crackling fire. I tried to ease my foot out of Red Hair-Ring's hand but as I moved, he tightened his grasp.

"*Psst!* Over here. Up, behind you."

I looked up into a nearby tree.

A short, blond-haired boy sat in a cage hanging from a branch. "Tickle his nose. When he sneezes, you can get free."

I picked a blade of grass and waved it under the troll's nose.

"Achoo!" Red Hair-Ring let go of my foot and scratched his nose, still sleeping.

I ran to the tree. "Who are you? What are you doing here?" I asked in a whisper.

"I'm Prince Alexander. They captured me and have been holding me for ransom. Help me get out. The cage door is tied to the tree limb above. If you untie it, the door will swing down and open."

I climbed up to the branch where the rope was knotted. Swiftly, I untied it. The door swung down, and the boy tumbled to the ground.

"Are you okay?" I whispered, landing on the ground beside Alexander.

"Yes, let's get out of here before they wake up. Follow me."

We ran for the shelter of the trees.

Alexander stopped. "Wait, I need to get something first."

CHAPTER 15

ALEXANDER dug in the mud at the base of a tree. He pulled out a dirty glob and wiped it on his pants, before putting it in his pocket.

I gasped. It was another one of the diamonds from the crown.

"This is important. The trolls were bragging about this stone and showing it to each other. Said it wouldn't be long before they had all the power they needed. Anytime a troll talks about power, something bad will happen. I watched where they hid this and decided I had to take it if I escaped. Let's get out of here."

He tugged my arm, and we headed to a path up the mountain.

After we had run awhile, Alexander stopped. Breathing hard, he looked at me. "Okay, so who are you?" He took a deep breath. "Where did you come from? You aren't Plumberian or Drainovian. Do you really come from a land beyond the mountain?"

I hesitated. Could I trust him? Maybe I should wait and just let him think what I told Red Hair-Ring was correct. "Ah, I'm David, a loyal subject of my ruler from a land far away."

"But where do you live? Why haven't I heard of you?" Alexander walked over to a small stream that trickled down the mountain. He bent over and cupped his hand to drink.

I followed, washed my face and hands and drank, too. I stood. "Well, I live in Edinville. We're a rather quiet people and like to keep to ourselves. We haven't traveled much beyond our borders. I'm the first of my family to be here." I relaxed. So far, that part was true.

"Well, David, I'm glad to make a new friend and ally for Plumberia. Follow me to my home. My father is King Thomas. He'll want to meet you and thank you for rescuing me."

We continued to climb the mountain path away from the sea. The trees thinned, and the air grew colder. I could see golden stars clearly above us. Though the moon looked like the one at home, the stars differed. They were not in any familiar pattern. The big dipper was gone and strange clusters shone brightly. Four bright stars shot across the sky.

"Look!" I pointed upward. "Shooting stars."

Alexander stopped and gazed above. "That's odd. We seldom see the stars move. Our learned ones say that most are stationary. It may be an omen. Let's hurry."

The moon and stars lit our way as we ran. Turning a bend, I tripped on a rock and fell, tumbling down the side of the mountain. Grabbing a branch from a bush, I held on as stones flew past me. My legs swung out and dangled behind me. I struggled to hold on. Cold sweat dripped into my eyes, burning them.

"David, I'm coming!" Alexander called. More stones rattled past me. "Give me your hand."

I reached up and grabbed his hand. He tugged me up without much effort. For a little guy, he was strong.

"Whew, that was close. Any farther and we'd be back with the trolls." Alexander looked at me closely. "Are you okay?"

"Yeah." I wiped my face with a scratched hand, and brushed the dirt off my clothes and hands. Most of the mud that had been caked on me had broken off in the fall. The button on the back pocket of my green pants was missing. I felt to make sure the diamond was still deep in my jeans pocket.

"Can you make it a little further? Plungerville isn't far from here."

"Lead the way." I followed slowly, watching for rocks. No way did I want to end up with the trolls.

"There it is." Alexander said, pointing to a group of lights ahead.

"Halt! Who goes there?" A sentry in front of a small brick house shone a light on us.

"It's me, Prince Alexander."

"Your Highness!" The sentry saluted him. "Oh, I'm so glad you're back. When you didn't report in from your peace mission, your father searched all over for you. We thought we'd have to go to war again against those miserable Drainovians to rescue you, but they denied having you. We've had no idea where you were ever since. Let's get you to the palace." He stopped talking as he noticed me behind the prince. "Who is he?"

"This is my friend, David. He rescued me from the trolls. They captured me, not the Drainosaurs. I've got lots to tell Father."

The sentry motioned to another soldier to stand guard. "We'll be at the palace. I'll return shortly." He opened the gate for us to walk through.

I followed them down a street. Tall pillars glowed faintly at all of the intersections. The buildings reminded me of old red-brick row houses in the section of town where my grandparents used to live. As we headed into a large grassy square, the moon moved from behind a small bank of clouds. Benches sat under trees near swings and water fountains. Beyond that stood tiers of seats surrounding a baseball diamond.

"Cool!" I said to Prince Alexander. "It's like the ball park at home."

"Yes, Pipeball is our favorite pastime in Plumberia. I was a pitcher before the War. Look! The palace is over there." Prince Alexander pointed to a dark castle-like structure past the ball field. Lights twinkled in a few narrow windows.

We ran the rest of the way to the palace.

A tall, wrought iron fence surrounded it. Sharp spikes poked up from the top of it.

"Who goes there?" a high-pitched voice called from behind the gate.

"It's me, Prince Alexander."

"Prince Alexander!" Keys clanged against metal, as a woman unlocked the door. "Welcome home. Let's take you to the king right away." Smiling, she patted the prince on his back and nodded to the sentry. "You can go back to your post now." She saluted the younger man and ushered us into the palace.

I noticed several tall thin light pillars on a table in the middle of a large square room. Six doors, two on each of the other three walls, opened at the same time. Out marched six men wearing blue suits.

"Your Highness!" They smiled and clapped their hands. Two men turned on more pillars on the table. A couple other men brought glasses of lemonade and slippers over to the prince.

I drank my lemonade and watched as two more men pulled a cloth off a large cage hanging above the center table.

Two beautiful large gray and white speckled birds began to coo. They sounded like the Stool Pigeons I had heard back on the beach near Drainovia. I wished I understood what they were saying.

"Hello, Brutus and Portia," said the prince, as he tapped on their cage. "I've missed you. Take a message to my father. Here." He scribbled a note on a small pad of paper that sat beside the light pillars on the table. Opening the cage, he placed the note in a small pouch attached to the leg of the largest bird. "Go to the King."

The bird flew out of the cage, circled the room, and disappeared through an open doorway.

"Brutus will return quickly. Smartest birds around and quicker than sending a waiter," said Prince Alexander, as he finished his lemonade.

"Where is Alexander?" a loud voice called. A white-haired man in flowing purple robes, nightcap and slippers, sailed into the room followed by the Stool Pigeon. "My son, you're back!" The king hugged the prince. Stepping back, he pointed at me. "Who is this?"

Prince Alexander pulled me forward. "Father, this is David. He rescued me from the trolls. He is from a land beyond the mountains."

The king's eyebrows rose. "Is that right? Hmm, I didn't realize anyone lived there. Well, lucky for us you were there to save my son. We are in your debt. Let's go into the dining room. Tell me what happened." He turned to the men. "Bring us some food and drink."

He motioned to a side room and let us enter first. "Have a seat."

The room had a large table with ten chairs. Behind it a china closet held dishes and sparkling glasses. A long narrow table sat under a window overlooking the front gate to the street.

The King wiggled his nose and looked at my dirty clothes. He pointed to a small room beside the china closet. "Maybe you would like to wash up in there."

"So," he said, turning back to the prince, "the trolls held you captive these last couple of months. We had scouts out as far as Drainovia looking for you. The Stool Pigeons reported back from Scarlet that you weren't there, so we feared the worst."

I took off the dirty vest and pants and rolled them into a ball. Then I washed my hands and made my way back to the table. I sat in a chair beside Prince Alexander and set the ball of clothes at my feet.

While the king and Alexander talked, I listened and thought. Were they talking about Captain Scarlet of the Drainovian Police? Did he work for the Plumberians? Why would a Drainosaur do that? I remembered that Oliver didn't like him. Maybe he sensed that something wasn't right about the Drainovian captain.

The king glanced at me, raising an eyebrow at my change of clothes. "Scarlet also said that the Drainovian crown was missing. They think we have it. How absurd!" He shook his head. "Those Drainovians are a selfish, suspicious bunch. If they took care of their citizens as well as they do their fancy machines, they would all be happier. Brutus came back a few minutes ago with a report that there was a ferret revolt this evening. Something about not having enough food."

"Father, if their crown is missing, isn't that why they are having internal problems? Isn't it linked to a legend about prosperity?"

The king rolled his eyes. "Bah! The Drainovians have so much head knowledge, but no heart. A country is only prosperous, if its lowliest subject is content and has his needs met."

A knock sounded at the door.

"Enter," called the king.

"Your food, your Majesty." A man set dishes on the table under the window. Then he turned and left.

"Let's eat. I'm sure you are hungry. David, try this cheese and rice dish. The cook always makes it with a little extra spice." The king rose and filled a plate. Then he handed it to me.

"Thank you." I took a forkful and found it both cheesy and delicious. As I drank from one of the goblets, peach juice dribbled down my chin. I wiped it with my napkin. The green beans, carrots, and stewed zucchini were also tasty. I would hardly touch the stuff at home, but now everything was wonderful.

"Why did the trolls keep you so long? I would've expected a ransom note or something from them. I'm thankful they didn't harm you." The king ate a forkful of vegetables.

Prince Alexander spooned up some rice and put it on his plate. "They fed me meat and tossed in a few vegetables every now and then. I was afraid they were fattening me up to be eaten. Red Hair-Ring said they sent a note by Stool Pigeon asking you for ransom. Didn't you get it?"

I almost choked. Those Stool Pigeons sure had their beaks into a lot of people's business.

"No," the king replied. "Knowing how stupid the trolls are, they probably lost the note or sent it to the wrong place. Brutus has been here, except when I sent him to Scarlet a couple weeks ago. You know, it did take him longer to get back than usual. I'll have to investigate this."

"I heard the trolls talking about power," the prince said. He reached into his pocket and pulled out the diamond. "They hid this stone under a tree. When we escaped, I dug it out and brought it with us. No way do we want trolls having any power."

"Let me see." The king turned it over in his hands. "I believe it's a diamond. Where did they get it?"

I leaned over to see. Suddenly, the diamond I had hidden in my jeans pocket burned against my backside, while the diamond in the king's hand began to glow. I jumped up, spilling juice down my jeans. My diamond popped out and flew at the diamond in the king's hand.

Shocked, the king dropped his diamond onto the carpeted floor with mine falling beside it. They glowed from yellow to a deep orange. Light flashed. A hazy holographic image of an old drainosaur appeared. It flickered and then faded.

CHAPTER 16

"WHAT was that?" Prince Alexander's eyes were large. "You didn't say you had a diamond. Are they both yours?"

I looked at the prince and the king. "Well, it's a long story."

The king scrunched his eyebrows together, like my dad did when he was suspicious. The prince just scratched his head.

The diamonds returned to a soft yellow color.

The king picked them up and set them on the table. "We have time to listen. You know, if that was a drainosaur, I'll bet the diamonds belong to them. I wonder if they are part of their missing crown. The trolls must've thought a diamond would give them magical powers to get food or something. They often think with their stomachs." The king drummed his fingers on the table, and then turned to me. "I think you need to be honest with us. What do you know about this?"

Should I tell him?

Something about the look in the king's eyes told me I could trust him. I rubbed a napkin on my juice-stained jeans and sat down. "I'm not from here. I come from above." I told them about dropping Mama's ring down the drain, my quest with Oliver to find the Drainovian crown, and collecting plumberries for the Psychedelic Caterpillar. "Then the trolls caught me." I looked at Prince Alexander. "You know the rest."

The king looked closer at me. "You were the topsider who fell into the lower drain with Princess Doris. Our lower drain cameras caught a few pictures, but you were covered with slime making it hard to see your face. I guess the walls are overdue for a cleaning. We access them from our basements."

I nodded and swallowed.

A knock sounded at the door. The king covered the diamonds with a napkin and then stood. "Come in."

A waiter entered. "Your Majesty, the sentry sent a Stool Pigeon with a message that says the trolls are at the outpost. They demand to see you. The sentry's not sure how long he can hold them off."

The king wiped his hands on another napkin. "Get the soldiers ready. Have the women alerted and equipped to march. Supply them with those new special weapons. If we can get the trolls corralled at the sentry post, we will be able to divide and conquer them. Then we'll see why they took Prince Alexander."

The waiter nodded and left.

The king turned to the prince. "Let's get changed. Your friend can go to a room and rest."

I straightened my shoulders. "Ah, Your Majesty, if it's okay with you, I'd like to help."

"If you wish. You'll need a uniform then." He glanced at me from head to toe. "I'll give you one of mine. Leave your dirty clothes, and they'll be cleaned." He picked up the napkin with the diamonds and set them in two different drawers hidden underneath the table. He used an old-fashioned key to lock the drawers. It looked just like my key. "There, that will keep these safe for now. No one will take them, especially with Brutus and Portia watching." He turned and walked out of the room. Alexander patted my back and pointed the way.

I left my dirty green clothes. Wearing my t-shirt and jeans, I followed. Somehow I would have to take those diamonds, find the third one and the crown. Maybe the King would help. If I put them all together with the crown, I could exchange it with the Drainovians for Mama's ring. Time was passing too quickly. I chewed my bottom lip. It was day two, and I had lost both diamonds to King Thomas. Things were getting more complicated. I wished I had Oliver and my teleporting hat. I wished I was home. Even arguing with Luis was better than this.

With a sigh, I walked with Alexander.

A few minutes later, wearing purple pants and jackets over black t-shirts, we headed out the gate to the stable. In the darkness a bird cooed, as the moon slid behind a cloud. Six women and six men, also in purple pants and jackets followed us. The women carried brooms over their shoulders. Dustpans hung from thick ropes at their waists. The men wore old west style guns in holsters in belts around their hips.

I expected to see horses waiting for us. Instead a row of large ostriches stood in front of a fence by the stable door.

"Everyone mount up." The king climbed onto the back of the tallest ostrich and picked up the reins. He prodded his mount forward. "Women, you are the only ones trained with the new weapons, so let's hurry up and get to those trolls. I don't want them to know what hit them. Men, if the new weapons fail, you know what to do."

They all nodded and got on their ostriches.

"Here, David. This is Winston," said Alexander. "He's big, sturdy, and steady. Perfect for you to ride."

I stuck my foot in the stirrup and swung up into a saddle, like I saw the others do. The ostrich eyed me and then pecked at my leg. "Ouch!" I moved my foot out of its way, almost falling out of the saddle.

"What's the matter? Haven't you ridden before?" Alexander grabbed my reins and gave a sharp tug. "They're stubborn. Let them know you're the boss. You'll get the hang of it. Give them one of these every so often, and you'll have them eating out of your hand." Laughing, he gave me a handful of small cookies.

I put all but one of the cookies in a pocket of my jacket and then gave one to Winston. He swallowed and nodded his head. I could have sworn he said *thanks*. I grabbed the reins. Using my knees like the prince did, I got my ostrich to move.

We surged forward. In no time we neared the sentry post.

There was loud yelling and the clunking of wood against metal. The sentry pushed against a metal gate, while a dozen trolls swung at it with wooden clubs. The gate and surrounding barbed wire fence sagged under the pounding.

The king held up his hand. We stopped. The women got off their ostriches, shouldered their brooms with the long handles pointing forward. At the King's command, the sentry ran from the gate and the women fired. Little darts flew out of the ends of the broom handles, up over the gate and down, hitting their marks. They reloaded darts from the storage boxes on the dustpans and fired again.

In slow motion, all of the trolls staggered, eyes wide, hands clutching their chests. One by one, they dropped onto the ground, snoring. The sentry hurried to open the gate for us.

"Okay, let's get them onto the ostriches and take them back to the palace dungeon." The king and another man hoisted Red Hair-Ring onto the king's ostrich, and then helped to gather the rest.

I couldn't believe how strong the Plumberians and the ostriches were. They barely flinched under the weight of the ugly trolls.

Alexander and I dumped a troll across his ostrich and fastened its hands underneath. He turned to help me load Winston.

"They sure stink!" I grunted, as we pushed snoring Blister up and over the back of my ostrich. "How long will they sleep?"

"They should be out for several hours," the prince said. "It depends on how much they weigh. We better hurry. Red Hair-Ring is the biggest. We don't want him awake before we get him in the dungeon." He tied Blister's hands together. "That should hold him for now."

I gave Winston another cookie. He grabbed it in his beak, tossed his head back, and swallowed it in one smooth motion. I thought I heard him mutter something, but I wasn't sure.

We headed back to the palace. We couldn't talk over all the snores.

As we approached the park, I noticed the sky was getting lighter. I bit my trembling lip, as I realized day three would be here soon and I still had much to do before I could return home.

Birds cooed and a Stool Pigeon swooped down to land on the king's shoulder. It carried something shiny in its beak. The king held out his hand and the bird dropped a sparkling stone into it. King Thomas glanced back at me and put the stone in his pocket.

Was that the third diamond? How did the bird, which looked like either Brutus or Portia, get it and from where? I tried to pull my ostrich closer to the king. Loud snorts and grunts sounded like Blister was waking, but then he relaxed and his snores continued.

I turned Winston through the side gate of the palace and stopped at a wide metal door.

The guard left her post to unlock the door, and we pulled the ostriches inside. The room was large. Small pinpoints of light glowed from the ceiling far above. A row of eight-foot square concrete block cells ran along the front and back wall. Each cell had a solid metal door with a four-inch window covered with a grate.

"Quickly, unload your prisoners into a cell and close the doors." The king opened one beside him, untied Red Hair-Ring and pushed him inside. He opened the next cell door and turned to me. "Get Blister in here."

I untied Blister and grunted, as we dumped him in a corner of the cell. No bed for these prisoners, I noticed. In a few minutes all of the trolls were safely behind bars.

"What happens when they wake up?" I asked the king.

"We'll question them." He turned to the men and women. "Take the ostriches back to the stable. Women, good job with the new weapons. Make sure they are cleaned and ready for use again."

The king pointed to Prince Alexander and me. "Let's go to my office." He patted his pocket and led the way.

CHAPTER 17

"WELL, boys, quite a night's work." The king sat at his desk and rubbed his eyes. "You should wash and rest for a few hours. The sun will be up soon. The trolls will be locked up when they wake and not have a clue as to why. They're a dumb lot. We'll see why they kidnapped you, Alex. They should know better than to go against me, but they never learn." The king shook his head.

"Come on, David. Let's get some rest," Alex said. "Father, please wake us in a couple hours, when you are ready to question Red Hair-Ring."

I saw the king remove the shiny stone from his pocket and put it into a box on his desk. That had to be the third diamond. How could I get it? It was now day three. I was running out of time.

The prince and I walked up stairs and down a long hallway to a door in the middle, facing the back of the building.

"Here's where you will stay. My room is next door. I'll wake you in two hours. Rest well." Prince Alexander opened my door and turned on a light. Then he waved and walked away.

I entered the room and closed the door. Light blue walls surrounded a big soft bed, a dresser with a mirror, and a chair. A gentle wind blew the curtains at the window, revealing thick metal bars. Safe or a prisoner, I wondered as I walked over and glanced down at a large trellis with roses twining up past my window. I breathed deeply of the scented air, trying to relax. At least I now knew where the diamonds were.

Yawning, I took off the purple jacket, pants, and t-shirt and put on a pair of pajamas that I discovered on the end of the bed. I stretched out under the soft cool sheets and slept soundly.

Scratching noises from far away got louder and louder. I woke and sat up. Looking around the room in the soft morning light, I remembered where I was and why. Rubbing my eyes, I saw a crab sitting on the ledge outside my window.

"David, I need yer help."

I rushed to the window. "Herman? How did you get here? How did you find me?" I helped the crab climb between two bars and put him on the bed.

"I came with my cousin to deliver a load o' sand. I been looking fer ye. Have ye heard 'bout the ferret revolt in Drainovia?" Herman squinted up at me.

"Yes, didn't that happen last night?" I stretched my arms over my head. They were a little sore from lifting Blister on and off the ostrich.

"It's been in the works for a while, but yesterday was the big revolt. One hundred ferrets marched into the royal kitchens and took control of all the food. The Drainosaurs didn't eat all day. Shoulda heard 'em grumble and moan! They negotiated and the ferrets won a few food concessions. But Captain Scarlet captured Oliver, who had just returned from helping the Psychedelic Caterpillar. He wants to make him an example. He plans to execute him today. Oliver said he knows where the crown is, too. Ye have to rescue him! All us crabs will help ye." Herman took a deep breath and his eyes bulged as he rubbed his pincer against his shell.

"Oh, no! We have to get back there fast. Poor Oliver." I bit my lip as I tried to think of a way to rescue him. More than ever, I wished I had my hat. Time was passing too quickly. I would have to get the diamonds, find the crown, and rescue Oliver in one day.

"Let me get ready." I splashed water on my face and dried it. The green baggy drainosaur pants, vest, and my t-shirt and blue jeans were clean and folded on a chair by the door. I dressed quickly in all of them. When I turned the door handle, it wouldn't open. Something definitely wasn't right about this. "Herman, the door is locked. Shh. I hear something. Hide in here." I picked him up and tucked him in my vest pocket.

"David, are you awake?" called a soft twittering voice. I heard a metallic scratching and a small ping. The door opened. An ostrich blinked at me, as a piece of wire fell from its beak. "I'm Winston. Remember me? Come on. We've no time to lose."

"I thought I heard you talk last night. Amazing." I shook my head. "How did you know I needed help? What's with the door being locked? Am I a prisoner?"

"Herman found me in the stable. He filled me in about what happened to Oliver. I met him before the war. He was such a friendly ferret. What a shame!" Winston eyed me. "When the waiters took your clothes to be washed in the laundry next to the barn, I heard them say which room you were in. So I told Herman. Some of the soldiers think you were working with the trolls and want to question you. As for the doors, well, the palace isn't completely remodeled. Your room used to be a storeroom, so it still has an old door. Now, enough talking. Let's go free Oliver."

I climbed onto Winston's back. I would get the diamonds when I passed the dining room off the big hall. Then I'd have to get to the office and take the third diamond from the box on the desk. We trotted the length of the corridor and down the steps to the main hall.

"Turn into the dining room. I need to get something I left there," I whispered to Winston.

I spotted the cage with the Stool Pigeons hanging above the table. One of them glanced at us and began chirping and flapping his wings. I leaned forward, putting my arms around Winston's neck. "We've got pigeon trouble," I whispered.

Suddenly a door banged open and a troll lunged for me. Red Hair-Ring had escaped!

"Let's go!" I called, ducking the troll's meaty hand.

People yelled from the rooms beyond.

I would have to return for the diamonds. Without them, I didn't stand a chance of getting Mama's ring from the Drainosaurs. Maybe we could hide in town and then sneak back in once the trolls were recaptured.

"Hold on." Winston dodged Red Hair-Ring again and ran for the door. As we sped past the Stool Pigeons, they both beat their wings and began to squawk louder.

Winston pushed open the door with his head, and we ran outside into chaos.

CHAPTER 18

AS we rushed outside, a dozen ostriches darted in different directions, knocking over a few guards. Winston and I headed for the gate.

I turned to look back as Red Hair-Ring bellowed and a dart zinged by me to stick into the troll's neck. He staggered and fell to the ground. A woman ran past me to stand over the troll. Several other trolls ran from the palace toward us.

The guards tried to get up to stop the trolls, but were knocked back down by ostriches trying to get away from the trolls. I heard King Thomas yell after us, as we ran through the park. We sped down a street away from the palace into the center of town.

People were beginning to stir. As we dashed down another street closer to the edge of town, I saw a woman outside hanging laundry. A dog barked and chased us a bit.

Climbing to higher ground, we slowed as we climbed a rocky trail. The mountain rose ahead of us.

Wet morning mists clung to the grass and made the stones slippery, as Winston picked his way up the mountain.

"Hey," I said. "I need to go back and get some things. Where are we going? This doesn't look familiar."

"We're going to rescue Oliver. We want to avoid Trollsylvania. King Thomas will have his hands full with the other angry trolls searching for Red Hair-Ring and his gang. I'll have a lot of explaining to do when I go back. I just couldn't see them blame you for the mess with the trolls and the prince's disappearance. What human in their right mind would ever work with them? I could tell when you fed me cookies, you were a good person. We're going up Rose Mountain. Watch out for the fairies. They hide in the mists and like to play jokes on anyone they see."

Herman poked his head out of my vest pocket. "Fairies really live here, eh?"

"Glad you came along, Herman. David may need your help." Winston stepped on a wet patch of grass.

I pulled Winston to a stop. "We have to go back to Plumberia before we rescue, Oliver." I told Winston a shortened version of my story.

"Promise we'll go back for the diamonds."

"Okay, I promise." Winston peered at the grass. "Uh-oh. Here come the fairies."

I looked down and saw the grass shimmer. Two tiny, sparkling, winged creatures appeared. A girl with flowing blonde hair wore a blue dress and silver sandals. A blond-haired boy dressed in a brown tunic with green pants and shoes fluttered beside her. They darted around the ostrich's feet, giggling.

Winston grunted and strained forward. "I can't move."

I tucked Herman deep into my pocket and leaned down toward the fairies. "Hey! Let us go."

The girl flew at my face. "You look different. You're not Plumberian like the ones I've done business with before. Where are you from?" She touched my hair and then tugged at my ear. "Come play with us," she whispered.

"Stop. That tickles." I waved my hand by my ear and shook my head. "I'm from another place. Let us go. I can't play."

The girl flitted in front of my eyes, laughing. "Of course, you'll play. You can't leave 'til you do." She flew to a nearby rock.

The boy tapped my shoulder. "Humor her. It'll be fun." He performed a mid-air somersault and landed beside the girl.

"I don't have time to play!" I yelled. "My friend is going to be executed in Drainovia. And I have to get home with Mama's ring, before I'm stuck down here forever!"

Gritting my teeth, I got down and tried to lift Winston's legs. Grass clung to them like sticky ropes, binding him to the earth. My fingers stuck to his legs. Now I couldn't get free.

The fairies doubled over, hiccupping in glee. "You should've played with us. You're really stuck down there now!" They fell into the grass, holding their sides as they laughed.

Herman climbed from my pocket. The grass hid his movements as he sneaked behind the fairies. He reached into his shell and pulled out a pincer of sand and tossed it at them.

Blinded by the sand, they sputtered as Herman grabbed them in his pincer. "Now, yer gonna let my friends go, ain't ye?" He shook them, until their teeth rattled and their wings drooped.

"We were only having fun," wailed the girl.

"Let us go and then we will," said the boy.

"No way. Do something or say some 'o yer magic words and let 'em go." Herman held them toward me.

"Fine. Spoil sport," the boy added.

The fairies mumbled some words, and the sticky ropes melted into the grass.

"There. Happy? Now let us go." The girl tried to wiggle out of Herman's grasp.

I walked over to them. Bending down I looked her in the eye. "Maybe you should stay with us, to make sure we get through your land safely."

"You'll be safe," she grumbled. "I give you my word."

"Yeah, but can I trust you?"

"You have to. Her word is good. She's Princess Ardis of the Rose Mountain Fairies and I'm Prince Klaus," said the boy, as he wiggled his wings. He slipped free and turned back to me. "But watch out for Reardon. He can't be trusted." He sparkled and disappeared.

I turned to the girl. "Princess Ardis, who is Reardon?"

"If I tell you, you have to let me go. This isn't fun anymore." The fairy princess pouted.

"First tell us. Then we'll let you go." I nodded to Herman.

"Reardon's my father's Prime Minister. He's evil and uses his power to make himself rich at our expense. I suspect he's planning something more devious than ever with his new Mountain Police. Look out for them. They are probably behind you and heading this way on their daily patrols. Now, please let me go." She wiggled her wings, as Herman released her.

She flew up beside me. "Reardon lives in the house just beyond the palace cave. He hates everyone who is not a fairy. Father finds him useful, but Father is King and more powerful. Watch out." She waved and then disappeared.

"Wait," I called, but it was too late. The air no longer sparkled around us. "Princess Ardis, we could use your help." I looked around hopefully.

I turned to Winston and Herman. "What do you think? Should we go back down the way we came or through Trollsylvania instead?"

"Between the Mountain Police and the trolls," said Winston, "the way we came and Trollsylvania are too dangerous. Let's head forward to the cave palace."

"Then let's hurry." I peered up the rocky path.

Winston nodded his head. "Let's befriend the fairies, as we go."

"Right, like I did with Princess Ardis." Herman chuckled, as he picked a piece of grass and chewed the end. "Will she come back?"

"It's hard to say. Fairies are an unpredictable lot. When you least expect them, they'll pop up, usually for mischief." Winston fluffed his wings and tail feathers. "If we follow this path, we should arrive at their palace. We can ask them to help us."

"I guess we have no choice. Herman, I'll put you in my pocket again. We might need a surprise or two to get through here." I pocketed him and climbed back on Winston.

The ostrich moved at a slow but steady pace. I glanced around at the rocks and bushes clustered around us. Nothing moved. Further ahead, a group of pointed rocks leaned over the path. The air was cooler with swirling, misty clouds. Goosebumps rose on my arms, making each hair stand like a sentinel. We rode closer to the overhang.

Something sparkled to my left.

"When you reach the rocks," a soft voice whispered, "go left and run into the cave."

An arrow zipped by my cheek. I yelped and ducked. Winston sprinted forward with me clinging to his neck. He zigzagged around bushes, and then ran left into a large cave and slid to a sudden stop.

I tumbled to the ground.

Herman fell from my pocket and rolled away.

CHAPTER 19

"THAT was impressive. Do you always make such a graceful entrance?" Princess Ardis giggled, as she flew around my head. "Welcome to the palace. You'll be safe here for a while. The Mountain Police saw you. If you're lucky, maybe they'll forget about you. But I doubt it."

She glanced out the large doorway. Then she pulled a cord. From a hidden cleft in the rocky wall a panel of woven branches, sprouting leaves and flowers, slid across the entrance.

I lay sprawled on a soft moss-covered floor and looked around. As my eyes grew used to the dimness, I saw tiny delicate wooden chairs and tables. I sat up next to a couch covered in light yellow flowers. Around the walls were balconies leading to little rooms with loosely woven grass curtains. Small glass jars hung from hooks beside the balconies. The light from the many lamps twinkled, making the room look magical. I stood to look closer and realized that lightning bugs sparkled inside the jars with twigs and leaves in their bases. A few flew out, going into other jars.

I brushed off my pants. Walking over to Herman, I pulled him from behind the carved wooden legs of a table.

"You okay?" I asked, putting him back in my pocket.

Herman rubbed his pincer on his shell and nodded. "Winston needs to get a better set o' brakes."

Soft laughter tickled my ear. Princess Ardis clapped her hands and Prince Klaus appeared. "My brother and I will help you get past Reardon's secret police." The princess flew to sit on a chair. "Father is busy at one of the High Council meetings on top of the mountain but Reardon is home, making life miserable for most of us. He likes to use his power to please himself when he knows no one will challenge him. Your only hope of getting by him is to stay with us. We'll make a plan. Hmm. If we help you, then you could help us with our problem." She pointed to the table and waved her hand, making a pitcher of water and several glasses appear. "But first, you must be thirsty after your journey."

Herman poked his head out of my pocket. "Water, did ye say?"

I set him on the table and tilted a glass to allow him to drink.

Winston sipped from a bowl, too.

I gulped some water and thought of home. Had they missed me? I needed to return today with Mama's ring. First, I had to get the diamonds and crown. Then rescue Oliver. Then return home. Maybe the fairies would help. I felt my stomach knot up again. Taking a deep breath, I tried to relax.

"Thanks. By the way, my name is David. This is Herman and Winston." I pointed to my friends. "What kind of plan do you have in mind? And what is your problem?" I sat on the floor, as Winston and Herman turned to listen.

"David, we could use your help to get rid of Reardon. We would be invisible and guide you with our magic so you would seem to have fairy power. That way we could get Reardon's bag of fairy dust away from his house, so his power would be gone and then we can get him removed as Prime Minister." Princess Ardis twirled in the air, showering sparkles all around. She sat back in her chair, crossed her legs, and grinned at me.

I shook my head. "We really don't have much time. I need to return to Plumberia for things I left there. Then I have to save my friend from being killed in Drainovia and return home."

Prince Klaus sat on another chair. He looked at his sister and then back at me. "It won't take much time. Then we'll help you."

Princess Ardis nodded.

"You promise to help?" Winston lowered his head and prodded Prince Klaus with his beak.

"We promise," said the prince and the princess together.

Remembering the strength of their sticky ropes, I recognized the advantage fairies could offer in rescuing Oliver. With their magical power, they could help me get the diamonds, too. "Well, what do we do?"

The fairies' faces lit up, as they clapped their hands.

Princess Ardis grinned at me. "We'll disguise you as a fairy, a very big one who comes from the mountain beyond ours. You'll give Reardon a gift, and in return he'll have to give you a special gift from his safe. We'll be invisible to follow him when he goes to unlock it. We know he keeps fairy dust in there. It was where we all stored our extra dust with our last Prime Minister. Now he uses it for himself. While he finds a gift, we will take the bag of fairy dust."

"Why haven't you done this before?" I asked. "Why do you need me? Why can't Prince Klaus pretend he's from another Kingdom?"

Prince Klaus cleared his throat. "Reardon is a large fairy, actually as big as you. We're not sure we could hold our own against him. With your size and our magic, you would be more believable as an important foreign fairy official. This plan gives him a reason to open his safe and a good chance for us to get the bag of fairy dust. Then we can discredit him when he has no power."

"You will be Sir David from the kingdom of Davidium. You can keep him busy, while we take the bag of fairy dust out of his house. We'll use that to help you save your friend. Without his fairy dust, Reardon will be finished. Brilliant plan, isn't it?" The smiling princess clasped her hands and leaned closer toward me. "How does this sound?"

I looked at Winston and then back to the princess. "Okay, but you must help me, too." I rubbed my cheek. "Who was aiming at us when we were coming up the mountain? Was that Reardon?"

Prince Klaus shook his head. "That was the crazy Mountain Police that Reardon set up several weeks ago. He said we needed to be safe from some evil Plumberians. We even have a curfew for our safety. I think he just wants us out of his way for whatever else he's planning. Usually, we can handle any Plumberians with our magic tricks. We haven't seen any in a long time, though. Not since their war with Drainovia."

Princess Ardis flew over to the far corner of the room and tugged a box away from the wall. Opening the lid, she pulled out a long piece of purple gauzy material. A silver belt fell onto the floor. Digging deeper, she tossed several pairs of pointed shoes with curved toes to me. Finally, she pulled out a silver crown with a dark blue sapphire set in the center.

"Here you go. We can use all this stuff. Come over here Sir David. Let's get you fixed up." Shaking the purple fabric, silvery sparkles scattered around the room. She sneezed. "Well, at least the fairy dust is still in this. We'll add a little more, and it should be perfect."

I walked over to her. "Isn't all this way too small for me?"

"Just a few adjustments, and it will work." As she swished the cloth back and forth, the length and width grew and swirled around, until it mounded gently over me.

I poked my arms and head through the fabric.

The princess tugged at the fabric on my shoulders and at my feet. "There's your royal robe." She tapped her fingers on my back and wings appeared on my shoulders.

"Whoa! How do they work?" I wiggled my torso and the wings moved back and forth.

"Use your shoulders to flex them. I don't think you'll have the strength to use them for flying. At least you'll look like a fairy." She snapped the silver belt, extending it to fit around me. "Put on this belt." She stretched the crown and handed it to me. Then paused to examine my ears. "Klaus, go get me the pizza cutter and pizza dough that the chef set aside to rise this morning."

"What are you going to do with pizza dough?" I asked.

"You need fairy ears. They need to be a little pointier than yours. Ah, here we go." Princess Ardis took the dough from her brother. Setting it on the table, she flattened two balls and cut large triangles and made a hole in the center. She held them out to me. "Now, put your ears through the holes."

I fit my ears through the holes. They felt heavy.

"Hold still while I smooth them in place." The princess lightly patted my ears against the triangles. She smoothed the dough to look as if they were part of my ears. "That should hold them. They look like fairy ears, don't you think, Klaus?" She flew back to admire her work.

"They'll do." He nodded and flew up to my head, tilting the crown. "That's better. If you set the crown like this, it won't knock off the pizza dough. Let's add a dark beard and moustache." He attached them onto my face with something sticky and then flew to his sister. "Very fairy-like, don't you think, Ardis?"

"Yes, I'd never recognize you now. Here." The princess placed shoes next to my feet. "The shoes are important. Hmm. Which pair should you wear?" She tapped her nose, looking at each pair.

I glanced at the tiny shoes. "The purple ones would match, I guess."

"Yes, the color would, but those are kicking shoes. You might need the red ones to make you invisible. What do you think, Klaus?"

"He definitely should wear the red ones." Prince Klaus tugged at the toes and heels of the red pair, making them big enough to fit my feet. "Try on these."

I stepped into them. The room flickered.

"Hey, where ye be, David?" Herman smacked his pincer on the tabletop.

CHAPTER 20

"I'M right here." I could see everyone. Why couldn't Herman see me?

"David, think heavy thoughts," said Prince Klaus. "Think about weighing as much as a mountain."

"Ah, there ye be." Herman squinted through a pair of glasses he'd pulled from his shell. Then he peered up at Princess Ardis. "How can I help ye, too?"

"You and Winston can make a distraction, so the Mountain Police won't be anywhere near Reardon's place." Princess Ardis' eyes twinkled. "I know. The captain really wants to leave and go to Plumberia to work in their stables. I can't imagine why though. Reardon and the other Mountain Police laughed at him. He's still mad about that. If you offered him a chance to prove he could take care of an animal like Winston, he'd be so busy trying to prove himself that everyone would watch."

"Yeah," Prince Klaus agreed. "Winston can make it difficult, so Reardon will keep trying. It should keep everyone entertained for a while." He looked at Herman. "You can be a representative of the Plumberian stables looking for new help with the animals."

"But won't Reardon want security to be on hand, if a visiting official comes into town?" I adjusted my belt.

Prince Klaus put some red polish on a cloth and rubbed the tips of the scuffed red shoes. "Contrary to what Reardon says about needing the police, fairies don't really need much protection. Because of your size, he won't expect you to have your own guards or need any security. He'll think you have even more magic than the average fairy. There. Your shoes will have a little extra power, since I polished them with red invisibility cream." Prince Klaus set the polish and cloth on a table.

Princess Ardis pulled out a photo album from a drawer in the table. She pointed to a tiny picture of a large mansion. "Here is Reardon's place. It's almost as big as the Plumberian palace, that I visited with Father. You'll fit nicely inside it. It is one of the oldest and biggest buildings in our land. I think the original fairies, who were almost as big as you, lived there. We've gotten smaller and our body systems have sped up over the centuries. That helps us fly faster." She closed the book and put it away.

"David, after you give Reardon the gift, you'll wait 'til he brings you a gift in return unless we need you. Keep him busy talking by making up stories about what's going on in your pretend Davidium. We'll do the rest, since we'll be invisible. When we tug on your robe, we can all leave. If you need to become invisible, tap your shoes together." She flew up beside my face. "Ready?"

Prince Klaus flew and pulled back the cover on the door. "First, Winston and Herman go out and come up the mountain making lots of noise. When the Mountain Police come, we'll head out the front and over to see Reardon. Let's go."

I set Herman on Winston's back. "Remember, keep them busy." I stepped away.

"I be the best caretaker o' these ostriches this side o' the mountain. Sit, Winston!" Herman clutched a few feathers in his pincer as Winston folded his legs under him and sat on the ground. Herman tapped Winston on his neck. "Up boy, stand at attention!"

Winston stood and turned his head to glare at Herman. "Don't overdo it with your tapping. I'll do what you want. I won't be quite as obliging to the captain, at least not at first."

"Good. We're all ready. Afterwards, we'll meet back here." I patted Winston's rump, and he trotted out the door.

A noise came from outside in the bushes.

"We be looking fer stable hands fer ostriches in Plumberia," Herman called.

High pitched voices and grunts with a few laughs erupted from beyond.

"Okay, our turn. Here is the gift. Father got it on a trading visit to Plumberia. Let's go." Princess Ardis handed a large golden vase to me and led the way. We headed out the front door and up a narrow rock-strewn street. The mansion loomed ahead.

"Remember, we will be invisible beside you. You'll still be able to hear us." Prince Klaus whispered. Then he and the princess disappeared.

I stood in front of a large ornate door and lifted a brass doorknocker. It sounded loud, as I hit it back against the door.

The door swung open, revealing a large, airy, sunlit room that covered the front of the house. Plush couches and chairs nestled around dark polished tables. I walked inside. Shimmering tapestries of mountain scenes hung along walls between tall windows at the front and sides of the room. Peering at one tapestry, I saw tiny fairies flying in and out of small huts alongside a stream. Toward the back wall between two wide doorways, a grand central staircase led to rooms on the upper floor. Fairies flitted all around, up and down the stairs.

"They are government workers," Princess Ardis whispered in my ear. "Don't stare."

"Who do we have here?" Two fairies dressed in matching blue uniforms flew up to me.

I stood tall and princely. "I am Sir David from Davidium. I would like to see Prime Minister Reardon. I come bearing a gift, so we might discuss friendship between our lands."

"Please be seated. We will announce your arrival." They pointed to a chair by the wall near the door.

Sitting straight, I waited.

"You are Sir David?" a familiar deep voice boomed.

I looked up into the eyes of Captain Scarlet.

CHAPTER 21

DRESSED in a long flowing red robe with his head covered by a huge hood, I recognized Captain Scarlet's round green face. His purple-edged wings looked droopy. What was he doing pretending to be a fairy Prime Minister?

Captain Scarlet, or Reardon, peered at me. His eyes narrowed. "Have we met before?"

I coughed and deepened my voice. "I have come seeking friendship with the Rose Mountain Fairies. We in Davidium have heard of your strength and power, and wish to be friends. Here is a gift to honor our intent." I gave a slight bow and held out the gold vase.

"Hmm. A worthy friendship, I'm sure. Thank you." Reardon's eyes shone with greed, as he snatched the vase from my hands. "I will bring your request to Parliament tomorrow. In the meantime, you must be my guest. Let me show you to a more comfortable room, where we may discuss matters. I also have a gift for Davidium." Reardon led the way to a room to the right of the stairs.

As we walked, I heard the murmuring of tiny voices and saw the air sparkle.

"You're doing fine," Princess Ardis whispered in my ear.

"Here we are. Make yourself comfortable. I hope this chair suits you. Most of the fairies here are small, so they make rather delicate furniture. Are all the fairies in Davidium as large as you?" Reardon smiled slightly, as he looked at me from head to toe.

"Yes. Does that bother you? I see that you are also large." I tried to speak coldly to let him know I thought he was rude.

"Why, yes. I am rather large as fairies go around here," Reardon sputtered. "I meant no offense. Please be seated. I'll be right back." He set the gold vase on a table next to a flowered sofa. He examined me again, as he turned to leave the room.

I sat in the chair beside the table, where I could watch the door. I felt a tug on my robe.

"*Psst!* David," whispered Prince Klaus. "The way he looked at you, I think he's suspicious. Come with me. Tap your toes on the floor, and you'll be invisible. Let's find Ardis."

Tapping my toes, I immediately realized that the prince was visible. "Hey, I can see you!"

"*Shh.* When you enter the realm of invisibility, you can see others who are there. Hurry. I think they went upstairs." Prince Klaus flew out the door and up the steps.

I followed as quickly as my robe allowed. At the top of the stairs, a light shone from the second room on our right. Entering what looked like a kitchen, I watched as Reardon opened a huge walk-in freezer. He entered, leaving the door ajar.

I saw boxes of frozen fish stacked alongside a wall. I gasped. Halibut! At the back of the freezer was a large black safe. Odd place for a safe. I supposed a thief wouldn't look there.

As Reardon inserted a key, he paused and twisted to look around. I held my breath, hoping he wouldn't know I was there. He turned back to the safe and opened it. He swung the door open wide enough for me to see stacks of gold bars, boxes filled with jewels, coins, and several bags. On top of one large box was a gold crown. It had three holes that must have once held gemstones. The Drainovian Crown! I had to get it, but how? Maybe I could inch over to it, snatch it, and hide it under my robe. Would it become invisible too? If not, I'd be in trouble.

"Ah, there it is," Reardon muttered. He reached down to pick up a gold chain with a red jewel hanging from it. "This will do nicely."

As he bent over, I grabbed the crown and hid it under my robe. At the same time, I saw a large bag disappear. I hurried out the door and ran down the steps. I tripped on the last step and fell in a tangle at the bottom.

The crown rolled under the edge of a tapestry near the door.

Visible now, I stood as Reardon came down the stairs.

"Oh, there you are," I talked loudly hoping that Princess Ardis and Prince Klaus heard me. "I just heard from one of your fairies that I'm needed back home. I must leave." Out of the corner of my eye, I saw the crown disappear.

"Let me present you with this as a token of our friendship." Reardon hung the chain around my neck knocking my left fairy ear to the floor.

"What? You are not a fairy! Imposter!" Reardon reached for my right ear and pulled off the pizza dough. "Mountain Police! Arrest him!"

I tapped my toes on the floor, turned, and ran to the now open front door, hoping I was invisible. To my relief, I spotted Princess Ardis and Prince Klaus, holding the bag and the crown by the door. As I sped by, they handed me the crown.

"Faster," Princess Ardis whispered. She flew in front of my face with Prince Klaus behind her carrying the bag of fairy dust.

I ran as quickly as I could. Soon we reached the cave palace.

"Whew! That was close." I collapsed onto the floor. "Do you think Reardon will come looking for us here?"

"Not yet." Princess Ardis paused in front of a pitcher of water on a small table. Turning, she handed me a glass of water. "Here. Drink up."

I gulped the water and handed her the empty glass.

Prince Klaus dropped the bag of fairy dust and sat beside me. "He'll be busy looking for his Secret Mountain Police to get them to do his dirty work." He nodded at the crown in the robe beside me. "What's with the crown? We saw you take it. It doesn't even have any gem stones in it and you already were wearing one. Why would you risk our plans for it?" He scowled at me.

I looked down at the crown. "Thank you so much for helping me. I thought I'd lost it when I fell! I've been looking for this crown." I told them my whole story. "Now if I can get the diamonds from King Thomas in Plumberia, I'll be able to trade the complete crown for Mama's ring and go home. After I rescue Oliver." I wiped sweaty palms on my pants and frowned. "But I have to hurry. Today is my last day. I must go home before midnight, or I'll be stuck here forever."

"We'll help you in any way we can," said Prince Klaus. He turned to his sister. "Right?"

"Yes, of course. But I don't understand how your Captain Scarlet can be Reardon." Princess Ardis clasped her arms around her legs as she sat in front of me.

Prince Klaus nudged her. "Think back, Ardis. He has only been here for one year. Remember when he first came? He brought gifts, told of ruling a far kingdom of fairies."

"Fairies, my foot," I snorted. "He's no more a fairy than I am." I scratched at my beard, peeling it off my face. The moustache was next. It felt good to be rid of them.

"That explains a lot. I can't believe we fell for his lies. I knew he was up to something, but to cripple Drainovia by stealing their crown and pretend to be a fairy to weasel his way in to a position of power here. Why, he's just evil!" Princess Ardis shuddered.

"I think King Thomas trusts him, too. He talked about sending messages to a Scarlet. He must mean him." I lifted the gold necklace from my neck and set it on the table. "Here, this should go to you two. It's probably stolen from someone. I can't imagine where Captain Scarlet or

Reardon got all that gold and jewels that were in his safe." I flexed my shoulders making the wings wobble. "Too bad I don't have time to learn to fly. These could be handy. How do I get rid of them?"

Princess Ardis flew behind me and tapped between my shoulders. There were sparkles all around me. Then the wings disappeared.

I slid the robe over my shoulders. "These shoes are cool. Can I keep them?"

"You like being invisible, huh?" Princess Ardis laughed. "Sure, until you have to go topside. We couldn't have our magic creating trouble in your world. As for the rest of what was in the safe, most of that is from our treasury and stored by the former Prime Minister who died right before Reardon arrived."

"I remember that necklace. It belonged to one of our early rulers. I saw it in our history book," said Prince Klaus.

Outside, a loud crash echoed.

CHAPTER 22

"OPEN up!" Herman yelled. "It be us!"

Prince Klaus flew to pull the cord to slide back the door as Winston and Herman stumbled into the room.

"Thought we'd never be rid o' those Mountain Police." Herman sighed.

"Yes, that captain is crazy." Winston fluffed his feathers and sat down, dumping Herman to the floor. "He had me trying to fly with his magic powder. Not that I got off the ground, but he tried. Now he thinks he's a great animal caretaker. He's leaving tomorrow for Plumberia."

"Argh," Herman pushed his pincer against the floor to right himself. "And the rest o' the Mountain Police agree, so we be pleased. They tried to keep us there and threw stones at us when we wouldn't stay. How did ye do with Reardon? Did ye git his fairy dust?" Herman rubbed his pincer against his shell and stretched.

"Well, we got that and more." I picked up the crown and set it on the table beside me. "Here's the Crown of Drainovia. Now, all we have to do is get the three diamonds and rescue Oliver. Oh, and by the way, Reardon is Captain Scarlet."

Herman's eyes bulged. "What do ye say? How can that be? Captain Scarlet is a Drainosaur, ain't he?"

"Yeah, but he wears a long robe with a hood. He has droopy wings too. He probably ties up his tail, so the fairies don't know he's a Drainosaur. He sure gets around. I wonder how he does it?" I scratched my face where the beard used to be.

"Reardon isn't always here. He goes on missions, he says." Princess Ardis rolled her eyes. "You know, I always thought he looked strange. For a fairy, I mean. Most fairies are slender and small. Now that I think of it, I don't think I've ever seen Reardon fly."

"That should definitely prove it. After all the lies he's told, Father will have to remove him as Prime Minister, because he isn't a fairy. I'll put his bag of fairy dust in our cupboard, so Reardon or Captain Scarlet or whatever you want to call him won't have any fairy power." Prince Klaus started to lift the bag.

"Here, I'll help." I picked up the bag and followed the prince to a room that was ten fairy-sized levels high.

"Put it in that cupboard, please." Ardis flew up and waved her hand toward an ornately carved cupboard at the back of the tiny room.

I reached in and set it inside. The cupboard disappeared.

The princess wiped dust off her hands. "There, safe and out of Reardon's way." She smiled.

I walked back to the others. "When he went on those missions, could he have used fairy dust?"

Princess Ardis shook her head. "Not likely. He'd need to use too much each time he traveled."

"He must have used a teleporting hat or maybe he was the one who used the crystal pillar in that cave." I sat back down on the floor.

"I'm not sure 'bout the pillar," said Herman. "I think the Plumberians used that. I doubt they'd be a tellin' a Drainosaur any o' their secrets."

"Would they go into Drainovia? Wouldn't they get caught?" I asked.

"You were disguised. Maybe they'd be, too."

"How soon do we leave?" I looked at the princess. "Since I can be invisible, can you help me get the diamonds?"

"Yes. Klaus go tell Father what has happened and have Reardon arrested."

I gulped down another glass of water. "Good. Then he can't execute Oliver. But if he has a teleporting hat, no amount of magic will hold him. Tell your father to take away his robe. The teleporter might be in his hood. It covered a large part of his face." I frowned. "If he knows you're on to him, he might already have gone back to Drainovia."

Prince Klaus headed for the front door. "I'll make sure Father knows what has happened and that we arrest Reardon."

"If he is in jail here," I said, "it will take time for the Drainovians to appoint another Captain. Oliver will have to stay in jail. Hopefully, we've given him some extra time. If he's in same tower they put me in, it will be easy to rescue him."

"On our way back to save Oliver, we stop in Plumberia an' git the diamonds." Herman tapped his pincer on his shell. "My cousin be still in Plumberia. He can help us if need be."

"Not to mention the rest of the ostriches. We'll be happy to help." Winston slurped at a dish of water.

"You know, I was wondering why you've helped us, since you belong to King Thomas."

Winston fluffed his feathers. "We try to help anyone in need. Those

Drainosaurs are a selfish bunch. Imagine not making sure their subjects have enough food." Winston burped. "Excuse me. Besides, King Thomas isn't so bad, just a bit misled. I'm thinking this Captain Scarlet has him fooled, too. When Prince Alexander went missing, Captain Scarlet showed up and said he would help us find the Prince. Said he had all kinds of power and could do this and that for us. All for a price, I'm sure. They used those Stool Pigeons to carry messages. What could the King do?" Winston stretched his long neck and used hit beak to scratch under a wing.

"Well, I'm glad you helped me get away. Red Hair-Ring was supposed to be in a cell. The way he came after me, I thought I was his next meal." I picked up the crown and slid my arm through it. I'd hold on tight to it before it disappeared again. "As far as King Thomas is concerned, you might be right, but he still has the diamonds. I'm sure he knows they're from the Drainovian crown."

"Do you know where the diamonds are in Plumberia?" the princess asked.

"I think so. If King Thomas hasn't moved them." I stood and picked up Herman to put in my pocket.

"Ready?" At my nod, Princess Ardis handed me a bag. "Here, you'll need these later." Inside were my sneakers.

I pointed to my feet. "Do I wear the red shoes to Plumberia?"

"Yes, they'll work all over Rose Mountain. But you can't wear them home."

"True. Thanks." I took the bag and put the crown inside with the shoes. Then tied it to a belt loop on my pants. "Let's go. We've got lots to do before midnight."

Princess Ardis flew out the door, as I climbed on Winston.

"Wait up!" I called, as we sped after her.

We zigzagged around some boulders and headed down the mountain. A soft breeze blew through the trees, rustling the leaves around us.

The smell of roses grew stronger, as we approached the gate. Spotting a sentry, I tapped my feet against Winston's belly to become invisible.

"Princess Ardis, wait," I whispered, but it was too late.

CHAPTER 23

"HALT! Who goes there?" The sentry called from her post. She held a broom, which I knew had sleeping darts.

With a wave of her hand, Princess Ardis sprinkled glitter in the sentry's eyes. The sentry sputtered, dropping the broom to rub her eyes.

The princess became invisible and flew back to me, landing on my shoulder. "Hold still, so Winston can get us through," she whispered. "The sentry shouldn't be suspicious of him."

The sentry blinked. "Hey, Winston, where did you come from? I could have sworn I saw one of those pesky fairies. Did you see anything?" She turned her head from side-to-side, blinking while she looked right through me and beyond.

I held my breath. It felt weird to know she couldn't see me.

"Pesky, huh," murmured Princess Ardis. "She hasn't seen anything yet." She flitted around the sentry's face, tapping her ears and then her lip.

The sentry smacked one ear after the other.

Princess Ardis giggled softly.

The sentry hit her own mouth. "Darn mosquitoes. They're nasty this time of day. Winston, where have you been? King Thomas was looking for you. He's also looking for that David. Guess he left when Red Hair-Ring and a few other trolls escaped. Broke right through their cell doors. Imagine that! There was a ruckus of some sort among the ostriches, too. What a time they had catching those trolls again."

Winston shook his head. "I went up the mountain early this morning. Nothing like fresh air to soothe and revitalize. Ever been up there?"

"Not recently. Been too busy with the trolls. King Thomas questioned them. Then sent all of them back, except Red Hair-Ring. He'll stand trial for kidnapping Prince Alexander. I don't like the idea of Red Hair-Ring staying here in jail. He's dangerous. He really raised a stink with King Thomas." The sentry laughed. "Raised a stink in more than one way, you know what I mean?" She laughed again at her joke.

"That's funny." Winston raised his beak to snap at a bug that flew by. "So what did the smelly brute do?"

"He accused Prince Alexander of stealing something from him. Of all the nerve!" She shook her head. "And after kidnapping the prince in the first place. Those trolls aren't very smart."

"King Thomas let the rest of them go?" asked Winston.

"Yeah, a couple hours ago. I think the king is going to watch them very carefully." The sentry rubbed her hands together. "The trolls had the nerve to spit at me when they went through this gate." She shuddered.

Winston eyed the road before him. "Is the king home? By the way, what did you say happened to that boy, David?"

"He just disappeared. Prince Alex was disappointed. King Thomas was a bit surprised. The Stool Pigeons were sent out looking for him, but they returned without any news. There is something fishy about him, especially since he ran away. Wish we could've questioned him." The sentry picked up the broom and set it against the wall of the building beside the gate. "I heard the king was going to visit some family in the city, when he got the chance. Might be this afternoon now that things have settled down."

"Hmm. Well, guess I better go home." Winston yawned. "I'll talk to you later."

The sentry waved him through.

Winston walked away from her and trotted down the road. "What do you think of that, David?" he whispered.

"I'm glad they arrested Red Hair-Ring." I leaned forward, holding onto Winston's long neck. "They'll have to double the door on his cell, so he can't escape again."

Winston ran through the town. No one was outside, and it was quiet as we neared the park across from the palace.

Princess Ardis flew in front of me. "Where are these diamonds you want to get?"

"They're in the palace in a dining room off the main hallway and in the king's office. We need to watch out for the Stool Pigeons, though. Look to see if their cage is covered. It hangs above the table in the middle of the main hall."

"The guard is eating." Princess Ardis pointed to the guardhouse. "Winston, drop us off at the front gate. We'll take it from there."

I slid from Winston's back and patted him. "Thanks, Winston, for everything."

Winston nodded toward my voice. "You're very welcome. Shout if you need me. I'll be in the stable. Hope I see, I mean really see you again when you aren't invisible or in danger." He fluffed his wings and trotted off.

As quietly as possible, I opened the gate. "Have you ever been here, Princess?" I whispered.

"Once, when Father visited King Thomas on a business trip. We trade goods now and then." She flew beside me, as we walked into the palace. She pointed to a cage above a small table. Inside it two Stool Pigeons were cooing. "They can't see us," she whispered in my ear. "Let's go find the stones."

Brutus gave a squawk and looked right at me. I shivered but led the princess past the table, opening a door into the dining room where I had eaten with Alexander and his father. The chairs sat around the sides of the table that was covered with a white tablecloth. The gold-rimmed plates and glasses sparkled in the afternoon light coming in the windows.

"This table has a drawer, right here." I lifted the tablecloth. Taking my old key from my pocket, I unlocked and opened the drawer. "I'm sure King Thomas put one diamond inside." Sliding my hand over the smooth wooden surface, I felt for the stone. My fingers curled around a large lump. "Here it is." I pulled it out, seeing it sparkle in the light and put it in my back pocket. "Now, look on the other side for a second drawer."

Princess Ardis flew under the table and lifted the tablecloth. "Over here, David."

I walked to her side and unlocked the drawer. After I found the second stone, I put it in my vest pocket.

"Hey, it's getting crowded in here." Herman stuck his head out.

I glanced down at him. "Shh. Hold onto it so we don't lose it."

"You said there were three diamonds, right? Where's the last one?" Princess Ardis sat on the edge of a plate.

"King Thomas has it, I think. I'm pretty sure I saw him put it into a box on the desk in his office." I glanced at the door.

Voices came from the hallway.

"I saw the door open your Majesty. It was like magic." A woman dressed in dark blue led King Thomas into the room. She was one of the soldiers who had gone with us to capture the trolls.

Thomas looked around. "There's no one in here. The door must not have been latched. It probably just swung open."

"Brutus squawked at the same time. He's the best guard we have. He misses nothing." The woman shook her head. She walked around the table, almost touching me.

I held my breath. The tablecloth was on top of the table and the first drawer wasn't closed all the way either. I hoped they wouldn't notice.

"Wait a minute. I know this wasn't open earlier." The woman closed the drawer.

The king hurried to her side. He opened the drawer and peered inside.

"Ah, so David is here. I knew he would come back for the stones." He ran to the curtains along the wall and pulled aside the drapery. "David, where are you? We have to talk."

The woman stared at the king. "Are you okay, your majesty?"

CHAPTER 24

WHAT if the king had just used me to get the crown for him? What if it was his plan for the Stool Pigeons to steal the crown?

"Don't tell him I'm here and don't tell him about the shoes," Princess Ardis whispered into my ear.

"David, I have the third diamond that you need." King Thomas walked to the open door and looked behind it. He turned back to woman and shrugged. "I'm fine. Well, I guess he's not in here anymore. We'll have to find him before that crook, Scarlet, gets here. He's due to arrive tonight." The king led the woman from the room.

"You haven't heard from him in the last few days, have you?" she asked.

"Not since Brutus arrived with his message the night Alexander returned." Their voices became muffled as King Thomas closed the door behind him.

"That was close." I tiptoed to the door, pressing my ear against it. "They're gone. We need to get to the office." I turned to see Princess Ardis still sitting, deep in thought. "Ready Princess?" I asked.

She glanced up at me and nodded. "Okay. When Father and I were here on business, King Thomas talked to us in a big room with tall windows overlooking a grassy hill."

"Yes, that's his office. It's on the other side of that large entrance hall."

Princess Ardis flew to the door and turned to me. "Then I know where it is, too. I'll head in first. What do you think about the king realizing that Scarlet is a crook? I thought he trusted him."

"Yeah, I wonder what made him change his mind? Hey, as long as we're invisible, we should be safe, right?" I looked at her.

She smiled. "We should be safe as long as they don't hear us or we don't move something that they can see. Let's go."

I opened the door, and the princess flew out.

I followed her back into the entrance hall past the table with the birdcage. Brutus and Portia were eating out of a narrow dish with their backs to us. Brutus raised his head. I held my breath until he dropped his beak back into his food. My heart pounded so loudly that I was sure the big bird could hear it. We turned down another hallway.

"Father, where is David?" Prince Alexander asked. "I thought one of the women said he was here?"

Turning a corner, I bumped into Princess Ardis who had stopped, sending her tumbling into a half-opened door where Prince Alexander stood. The princess just missed him, as she hit the door and slid to the ground. She lay there not moving. The air around her shimmered and she suddenly became visible.

I gasped, as Alexander kneeled to look at the princess.

"What have we here?" King Thomas got up from a chair behind a desk covered with papers and books. He walked over to her tiny figure. "Is this little Princess Ardis?" Bending over, he picked her up and placed her on a leather sofa at the side of the room.

Alexander stood beside his father. "What is she doing here? Was she invisible?"

"Yes, she was. Maybe David is with her. If he is also invisible, that could be why we missed him." The king scratched his head.

The king waved a tissue in front of Princess Ardis' face. "Alexander, we have to warn David that Scarlet is trying to take over Drainovia. If that happens, David will never get home. As a whole, the Drainosaurs might be a stubborn and selfish lot, but they aren't nearly as evil as Scarlet." King Thomas smoothed the princess' hair out of her eyes. "Alex, did you know Scarlet was behind the trolls capturing you? He bribed them with food. He conned Brutus and Portia into stealing the Drainovian crown, too. Said he would find you, Alex, if they did it. The Stool Pigeons fooled him though. They hid the diamonds and left clues for us to find them. David and Red Hair-Ring found them first, though. Scarlet has been looking for the diamonds since. A lot depends on finding the crown and returning it to Drainovia. It could be our key to get Upper Drain rights."

Ah-ha! The king wanted to use the crown to gain access to the Upper Drains. I had to get all three diamonds, return to Drainovia to rescue Oliver, and convince Princess Doris to give me Mama's ring. Time was running out. It was early evening. I only had until midnight.

My hands shook. I took a deep breath, trying to relax.

Alexander folded a tissue and placed it under Princess Ardis' head. "I'll bet Scarlet thinks the trolls still have me as a prisoner."

"He'll be surprised then. I'm just glad we have the three diamonds, or at least we have one. I think David has the first two. The one we have is the biggest and I believe most important, possibly the key to the power of the crown." The king went to a drawer and pulled out a small vial. "Here are the smelling salts. Let's see if a whiff of this will help the princess." He walked back and waved it near her nose.

She coughed and pushed the vial from her face. Sitting up, she rubbed her forehead.

"Welcome, Princess Ardis," said the king. "To what do we owe this pleasure?"

She coughed again and glanced around the room. "Ah, um, I was looking for someone."

I remembered that the princess couldn't see me now that she was visible. Spotting a box on a desk, I tiptoed to it and lifted the lid. As I reached in to pull out the large diamond, the lid closed on my wrist, holding me tight.

CHAPTER 25

"NOT so fast, David." King Thomas held the lid down on my wrist. "We need your help and you need ours. Let's work together."

My heart was heavy at being caught. I reappeared. "What choice do I have?"

King Thomas looked me in the eye and released my arm. "We all have choices. We'll have to trust each other, if we want to succeed in both our missions."

"What do you want?" I dropped down on the sofa beside Princess Ardis who flexed her shoulders, wiggling her wings.

"It was my father's dream to go topside and discover our roots." King Thomas pulled a chair to sit across from me. He motioned to the door. "Alex, a servant has gone to get me some coffee. Close the door before he gets back. David, if we have the crown, we can trade it for Upper Drain rights."

I shook my head. "But I need it to get my mother's ring back and go home. The Drainovians think her ring is their crown."

"That's the beauty of my plan. If we return it to them together, for what we both want, they'll have to grant our wishes. By now they must know they don't have their crown and that you were right. They'll be very anxious to get the real crown and restore their power."

"How do we do this? Will they just let us walk in and announce we have their crown?" I raised my eyebrows in disbelief. "They'll just take the crown and arrest us."

"Hmm. We'll have to watch out for Scarlet, too. By the way, he's due here tonight. He thinks I'm helping him take over Drainovia in exchange for freeing Prince Alexander. He doesn't know the prince escaped." The king shook his head. "As if I would truly trust Scarlet."

"My father has Scarlet in our jail on Rose Mountain," said Princess Ardis. She explained what had happened.

"He tried to masquerade as a fairy?" King Thomas laughed. "He's as different from a fairy, as I am from a drainosaur. He's a very greedy, dishonest character. Let's hope your father found his teleporting device." He turned to me. "Do you have one of those special hats?"

"I left mine back in the cave near the crystal pillar."

King Thomas nodded. "You found the cave? I thought we'd hidden it pretty well from outsiders. At least we know where your hat is."

I leaned back on the sofa and nodded. "Oliver and I found the cave. Gert and Trudy, the Psychedelic Caterpillar, told us how to use the pillar after I had broken their cocoon. We used it to go to the plumberry bushes in Trollsylvania. They needed more berries to remake their cocoon. I hope they were successful."

Alex looked surprised. "So that's how you found me."

I nodded. "Red Hair-Ring caught me. Everyone else managed to hide in the mud by the tree. A 'sending place' Trudy called it."

"I know it," said Alex.

King Thomas looked at the bag dangling from my waist. "Did you find the crown?"

I patted the bag. "Yes, Scarlet had it in his house on Rose Mountain. Brutus left clever clues. I'm glad Herman and Oliver could read Pigeonese. Speaking of Oliver, we really need to rescue him. And I have to get back by midnight. Let's get moving."

"Arrgh, I'm comin' out now. Are ye done talkin' an' ready to go? What's our plan?" Herman popped his head out of my pocket.

I reached in and set him on the nearby desk. "How about this, we could all dress like Drainosaurs and return to Drainovia in disguise."

King Thomas shook his head. "Maybe we should try a more diplomatic way. Send a message about finding the crown. Say that we would like to give it to them in exchange for David's mother's ring and Upper Drain rights. We'll have to tell them that their own Captain Scarlet was behind the theft."

"We could split up the diamonds in case they take us prisoner. We'll have a diamond and the crown. King Thomas, you bring two diamonds." I reached into my pocket and then set a sparkling stone on the desk. "Here's one of them."

"Portia could take a note and Brutus could follow with a diamond as proof of what we're telling them," added the king. "Take the brooms and dustpans, too."

"A little fairy dust might help," said Princess Ardis. "I'm going with you."

"After you send a message and a diamond by the Stool Pigeons, we'll head out," Alex said. "You know where everything is in Drainovia, right, David?"

"If he doesn't, I do." Herman tapped his pincer hard on the table.

"I think this might work. When we all get together, we'll have the whole crown for them." King Thomas rose as a knock sounded on the door. "Come in."

A servant entered carrying a tray with a coffeepot and mug. "Your coffee, Your Highness." He set it on a table.

King Thomas followed the man to the door. "Have Brutus and Portia ready for a trip."

"Of course." As he started to close the door behind him, he twitched his nose and sneezed, falling back against the door.

The air shimmered and suddenly Prince Klaus appeared. "We have trouble." He collapsed on the sofa beside his sister.

CHAPTER 26

PRINCE Klaus struggled to catch his breath. "Reardon, or your Captain Scarlet, has escaped."

Princess Ardis leaned toward her brother. "Relax. Take a deep breath, and tell us what happened."

"The guards apparently misunderstood Father's orders. They were looking in his palace for a teleporting hat. They didn't think to take his robe. When they went back to his cell, he was gone." The Prince closed his eyes. "I came as quickly as I could."

I jumped up. "Where would he go first?"

King Thomas groaned. "He is due here tonight. We'll have to work fast. I'll send the Stool Pigeons to Drainovia. Let's get ready to go."

"The crabs o' Crabenda be at yer service, too." Herman smacked his pincer against the table.

"Here, back in you go." I scooped Herman into my pocket. This time he was on top of the diamond. "Hold on and don't fall out."

Alex turned to me. "Stay with the plan. Let's meet at the Drainovian Palace in two hours. We can go by way of the pillar of Lady Scarlet."

Princess Ardis flew up beside my face. "Go and get ready. I'll fill in Klaus about our plan. You'll need both of us."

In his room, Alex and I took two different sized pillows and stuffed them into the green pillowcases he found in a drawer. The prince dressed in green pants. He stuffed one pillow under his shirt and in his pants. Then he put on a green coat. The second pillow he pinned on as a tail.

"You look pretty drainosaur-ish." I laughed and poked Alex in his pillowed stomach. "Let's go."

"What is this?" I held up a couple miniature brooms with dustpans stuck to their tops that were on the dresser.

Alex tucked one broom into his pocket. "You keep one. They're just a couple truth darts I made back in school. They might come in handy."

"Show me how to use them," I said.

Alex slid aside a small door on the dustpan to take out a tiny dart as big as a matchstick. Inserting it into a hole in the pole of the broom, he touched a button near the straw base.

"There, all set. It fits neatly into your palm so no one can see it." Alex held it out to me.

Taking it in my hand, I studied it carefully. "Is there a safety on it, so I don't accidentally fire it?"

Alex grinned. "Sure, right here." He touched the button near the base. "If it's out, it's on. When it's in, it's off."

I carefully placed the miniature broom with dustpan deep in the back pocket of my green pants. "Does this stuff work? Make a person tell the truth, I mean?"

"Yes, we used them during the war," said Alex.

"Be sure ye put them far from me." Herman shook a pincer at me. "I don't want to be jabbed."

"No problem." I turned to Alex. "Let's go find your father."

We headed back to the king's office.

"Alex, I've sent Portia on her way. Brutus will leave shortly with another diamond in a special see-through pouch that can only be opened or removed with a key that I will bring. If anyone attempts to harm them, the birds will return here. I will leave right after you." The king held out his hand to me. "Here's a backpack for the crown."

"Thanks." I took the bag from my belt and set it inside the backpack. Then I swung it across my shoulders. "What about Scarlet? We have to make sure we beat him to Drainovia. I can't let him kill poor Oliver." The clock on the wall struck eight p.m. It was only four hours until midnight. I bit my lip. I was anxious to return to Drainovia.

"Let's go to the pillar room." Prince Alex motioned for the two fairies to join us.

We walked through the hall and then down a narrow flight of steps that led to a locked door. Using a key like the one I had used to open the door in the cave, we entered a dark, cool room. A large crystal pillar glowed before us.

"What are the crossing words?" a familiar female voice asked.

"Four for the crystal cave." Prince Alex held my arm as Prince Klaus, and Princess Ardis sat on our shoulders. Lights flashed and whirled.

Closing my eyes, I fought the swirling sensation in the pit of my stomach. Suddenly, it was dark and still. I smelled damp salty sea air and could hear waves lapping on the beach.

"Lights, please." Prince Alex clapped his hands. The pillar in the cave brightened.

Seeing my pillows and hat on the shelf where I had left them, I ran, nearly tripping over a soft cottony mass. "Oh no, Trudy's and Gert's cocoon," I moaned. "I'd hoped they'd made a new one."

Herman poked his head out of my pocket to examine what I'd found. "What a terrible shame!"

Alex glanced at his watch. "We have four hours 'til midnight."

"I need to get Mama's ring and go home. Let's go." A few minutes later, with me wearing the pillows and holding the green-bean hat, we left the cave.

I pushed some brush over the entrance of the cave to hide it again. The moon shone brightly, reflecting off the water and lighting the landscape. "Let's follow the beach and head back toward Drainovia. We have to watch out for the Marsh Fellows. If we avoid them, we should be fine all the way to Crabenda."

"Yep. Then it be just a rock's throw or so to Drainovia." Herman jiggled inside his shell. "Won't be long now."

We walked along the sandy shore, until the reeds grew thick and close. Princess Ardis and Prince Klaus flew at my side.

"Look, Mommy! There's David and his friends." A giant frog hopped in front of us. I recognized her as the young female frog.

Mommy frog joined her. "What a nice time for a visit. You missed a very tasty dinner, David. Those beans were fantastic."

"I was on an important mission. My friends are here to help me." I glanced around, looking for the rest of her frog family.

"We want to help you, too." Mommy frog leaned over and placed a long arm around my shoulders. Her bulging wet eyes reflected the moon. She blinked and seemed to drip moon-drops onto my face.

I shuddered, holding out my hands and stepping away. The fairies became invisible.

Herman popped out of my vest pocket, waving his pincer. "We're off to save the ferret, Oliver, from being executed in Drainovia."

I shoved him back inside.

"Lead the way. We will do all we can to help." Mommy frog called to her family, and they hopped out of the watery reeds.

"Are you sure they should follow us?" Princess Ardis whispered.

I shrugged. "If nothing else, they'll provide a distraction."

We walked down the shoreline until we came to the sandy beach of Crabenda. Herman waved at a couple crabs as we slowed our walk. The crusty crabs scuttled out of our way. "Herman's back! He's got David and the Marsh Fellows."

Scritching and scratching across the sand, Grandpappy stopped in front of me. "Have ye heard 'bout Oliver? They have him in the Tower.

They be piling on as many charges against him as they can, 'cause he's been caught stealin' food from the kitchens before. Want to make an example o' him." Grandpappy shook his head. "Don't look good fer him."

"We're on our way to rescue him," I said. "And barter with the Drainovian King."

Herman waved his pincer at my backpack.

Grandpappy chuckled. "Who all be with ye?"

Setting Herman in the sand, I introduced the two fairies who were visible again and Prince Alex.

"Nice to meet friends." Grandpappy glanced at the Marsh Fellows who were splashing each other in the water. "What 'bout them?"

I rolled my eyes. "They want to help."

A small crab moved beside Grandpappy. "I saw the Stool Pigeons go by here earlier. They were headed for Drainovia, too."

"That would be Brutus and Portia, my father's messengers," Alex said.

The crabs coughed and sputtered, tossing spurts of sand at Alex.

"Ah, they've had some bad experiences with Stool Pigeons lately." I brushed the sand from Alex's tail pillow.

"We just ousted Roscoe and his Stool Pigeon henchmen from power. Nasty bunch," said Grandpappy. "David, that information and stone helped us. Thank ye. We best be gittin' along to save Oliver. Onward!"

A scurry of sand shot out, as a dozen crabs clambered to the surface.

"Forward, crabs." Grandpappy raised his pincer for them to follow.

Our strange procession worked our way down the beach. The pile of rotted fish appeared. White bones sprouted from the sand. The stink didn't seem as bad as before, maybe because the smell from the lemon trees so popular in Drainovia was stronger. We were getting close.

I heard a siren in the distance. Something was happening. We climbed up the bank onto a grassy knoll.

The city of Drainovia lay ahead. Lights flickered in many of the windows. Flying doors loaded with Drainosaurs swooped down near the gate to the city.

Goosebumps raised the hairs on my arms. We marched on, picking up our pace. A familiar Drainosaur spotted us, as we neared the entrance.

It was Captain Scarlet.

CHAPTER 27

"STOP them!" From atop a flying door, Captain Scarlet pointed his bony fingers at us.

The nearest group of Drainosaur soldiers flew toward us on their doors. They waved glowing sticks that spewed little lightning bolts in all directions. Hordes of flying Hand Cuffs followed.

"Watch out for the sticks, and those Cuffs are really strong," I yelled. "Princess Ardis and Prince Klaus go with Herman to the Tower and free Oliver. Alex, follow me to the palace."

I waved goodbye to Herman, Grandpappy and the other crabs.

Captain Scarlet pulled out a large glow stick and fired it at me.

Alex and I ducked and rolled under a tree. A lightning bolt sizzled in the leaves above us.

A sudden breeze blew through my hair.

Looking up, I saw an enormous dark butterfly swoop down. Sparkling dots flecked its wings, and antennae wiggled from two heads.

"David, we're here to help you. Climb on." Trudy and Gert smiled and nodded at Alex. "Bring your friend."

"Yay! You made it!" I climbed on their fuzzy, glow-in-the-dark thorax and abdomen. I pulled up Alex to straddle behind me. "Get us to the palace. We have to find the king and rescue Oliver. Please hurry."

"You mean, Queen Doris, don't you?" asked Gert.

"Oh, yeah. I forgot they were preparing for a ceremony to make her queen." I leaned forward a bit and held on behind their heads.

We flew up as lightning bolts snapped and crackled around us. I saw the frogs hopping and bouncing the Drainosaurs off their doors, as if they were ricocheting balls in a pinball machine. The frogs laughed and waved, as they bowled over the remaining Drainosaur soldiers. The bolts didn't even faze the Marsh Fellows. I smiled. They weren't so bad after all.

Captain Scarlet zoomed away in the direction of the palace.

"Faster! We have to get there before he does." I pointed out the Drainosaur to Gert who nodded.

"We will beat him." Trudy swiveled her head to look for a safe spot to land at the palace. "Go in this door by the upper parapet."

"We'll wait in case you need us." Gert and Trudy sat down. Trudy bent over and used her antennae to tie the laces on one of their slipper-covered feet.

"Thank you so much." I patted Gert's smiling head.

Alex scrambled off behind me and we headed to the door. Fortunately, it was unlocked. We opened it and tiptoed down the stone steps to a door at the bottom. Turning the gold handle, we entered a large sitting room.

Queen Doris stood with her back to us at a table near a window. A small glowing pillar on her desk lit the room. She was sorting through piles of boxes and muttering under her breath. "It has to be here. Where did it go?" She pulled a book from a box. "This will help. The old ones knew so much." She flipped through dusty pages and sneezed. She stopped to read a page. "Oh, no. I was afraid of that. The crown I have *is* fake." She plopped down on a nearby chair. Glancing up, she spotted us. "You!"

I walked over to the Drainosaur. "Did you get the message from King Thomas from Plumberia?"

"Yes, and I have seen the diamond. It seems you were right. I do have your mother's ring. I was so hoping that you were wrong. Do you have the rest of the stones and the crown?"

Prince Alex stepped forward. "I'm Prince Alexander of Plumberia. Your Captain Scarlet has deceived you."

The door opened, slamming against the stone wall. Captain Scarlet stood holding Brutus by the neck. The Stool Pigeon squawked, flapping his wings against the bony grip. The clear protective pouch holding the diamond sparkled with every move. Captain Scarlet walked over to us waving the struggling bird. "Not so fast. I have your diamond and the power is mine. I will be King! You can't stop me."

My hand felt the truth dart in my pocket. I yanked it out, released the safety, and fired at the captain. The dart stuck in his neck.

Another gray bird flew through the window. Portia clawed at Captain Scarlet's head, leaving bloody scratches.

With a yell he dropped Brutus. Staggering around the table, he swatted at Portia who pecked at his head. He tripped over a box, fell against the window ledge, and then toppled out.

"Eeeeeee." Scarlet's scream ended with a thump.

CHAPTER 28

PRINCE Alex and I ran to the window and peered down.

Gert and Trudy flew into view. Captain Scarlet hung on them. His beady eyes squeezed tight in his sickly, scratched face.

"Where do you want him?" Gert and Trudy fluttered at the window.

Queen Doris stood with her fists balled tightly on her hips. "Take him to the Tower on the right. We will meet you."

I heard trumpets. In the moonlight I saw King Thomas and his advisors climbing up from the beach and heading toward the city gate.

Queen Doris pointed to the newcomers. "I see we have much to discuss."

The Stool Pigeons flew to Prince Alex's side, cooing and clucking.

Alex patted them. "Yes, Brutus, everything will be fine."

"Let's get to the Tower." Queen Doris led us out through a hallway and into the room where I had first met the old king. The room sparkled with all its golden drapery. Lemons sat in bowls all around. She opened another tower door.

A dozen crabs dropped pebbles on us from above.

"Hey, stop! Herman, it's me." I waved at Herman and the other crabs.

Queen Doris touched a small pillar on the wall, shedding light to the top of the stairs where two Drainosaurs sat tied together by thin fairy-spun threads. Princess Ardis and Prince Klaus flitted around their heads. The Drainosaur guards tugged and twisted, trying to escape.

Queen Doris glared at the two guards. "What are you doing here? I fired you last week when you helped the ferrets steal from the kitchen."

One Drainosaur stuck out his chin and snorted at the queen. "We're not talking. Ask Captain Scarlet."

The other whined, blaming the first one for getting him in trouble.

"Be silent!" Queen Doris roared. "I will deal with you later."

Crabs skittered across the floor, trying to get out of the way of the queen's tail, as she swished it back and forth.

I ran into the moonlit tower room. "Oliver, are you here?"

The ferret looked up at me from a cot. Then he leaped into my arms. "David, I'm so glad you're back."

I hugged him. "I'm so glad you're safe. I've missed you."

Gert and Trudy flew in through the window. Captain Scarlet fell off their back onto the floor. The Cuffs flew in and surrounded him.

"I wanted to rule. I deserve to be King." Captain Scarlet knelt on the floor, his head in his hands, whining and sniffling. Rolling to his feet, he spotted Oliver. "You! I planted enough blame against you to keep me in the clear. You will hang for my deeds." He clamped his fingers over his mouth, trying to stop the words. "I did it all. I forced the Stool Pigeons to steal the crown, but they tricked me! They hid the diamonds. I had the trolls kidnap Prince Alex, too. Yes, it is all supposed to be mine! Mine!" With a groan, he dropped onto the cot and shook his head.

"You are under arrest for treason. You will remain here until your trial." Queen Doris threw a box of bandages from the desk drawer at Scarlet. "Here. That's more than you deserve." She turned to Oliver. "You are free to go with my apologies."

Oliver swaggered over to her with his front paws hooked in his overalls. "'Bout time, Queen. A little restitution would be appreciated too." He twirled his tail and patted his stomach.

Queen Doris nodded. "We will have to consider kitchen privileges for you and your family, perhaps?"

Oliver smiled. "That's more like it. I think that will be fine."

The queen turned to Alex. "Prince Alex, shall we receive your father and the rest of his group downstairs in the assembly room?" She glanced at me. "David, I believe I have something you might want."

I nodded, daring to hope she would return my mother's ring to me.

We trooped down to the large golden assembly room. Crabs sat under tables, the fairy princess and prince sat on the edge of a lemon bowl. Doors opened wide as trumpets announced King Thomas and his advisors. He carried a small, jeweled box and set it on a table in the center. Brutus and Portia flew over, landing on King Thomas' shoulders.

At the wall Queen Doris moved a picture of lemon trees to the side and opened a safe. She pulled a blue velvet bag out and set it on the table.

"Welcome King Thomas." Queen Doris nodded at him. "I understand you have something for me?"

CHAPTER 29

KING Thomas commanded the birds to sit on a table at the side of the room. He unlocked the pouch on Brutus and took out the diamond. Then he opened the jeweled box to take out a small parchment and a second diamond.

"Yes, here are two of the diamonds. I also would like to return the Building Codes that an old one had taken from you long ago. It is a gesture of good will. In return, I ask that we might share Upper Drain Rights." He handed both to the queen.

She smiled, as she gazed at the diamonds. Looking at the parchment, her eyes widened. "I was looking for this, among other things, today. Thank you. I think that is fair. I will have the royal secretary record it in the *Royal Ministry of Stairs and Records*."

Sliding the backpack from my shoulders, I took out the real crown and handed it to Queen Doris. "Here is your crown." Reaching into my pocket, I pulled out the third stone. "And here is the last diamond."

I set it on the table beside the other diamonds. They began to glow and pulse. A Drainosaur appeared in swirls of light. Words, symbols, and figures flashed in a rainbow of colors, circling the room.

Queen Doris gasped. "The power remains! They are the diamonds and the crown of Drainovia." She placed the diamonds in the crown and then put the crown on her head. It almost slid down her face. "I guess this one is too big for me. Father only wore it for special ceremonies." She set it into the wall safe.

She handed the velvet bag to me. "Here is your mother's ring."

I opened it, pulling out the crown-sized ring. Yellow rose cut diamonds winked in the light. "Oh, thank you!"

"We must celebrate!" The queen clapped her hands.

Then a clock chimed twelve.

I couldn't hold my feelings inside any longer. Hot tears ran down my cheeks. How could I have forgotten the time? I would be stuck here forever! Mama wouldn't get her ring back, and I would never again see my family or friends. I had come so far and done so much, only to have lost everything. I missed Mama. Even Luis didn't seem so bad after all I'd been through. What would I do now? I plopped into a chair and buried my face in my hands.

"Oh, David, I'm so sorry." King Thomas rose and put a hand on my shoulder. "You are welcome to live with us."

I turned my wet face to him. Looking through watery eyes, I tried to smile. "Thanks. I just wanted to go home so much. I finally have Mama's ring, and now she'll never get it back."

Sniffling, I stood, unpinned my tail pillow and set it on a small table. Then I took off the rest of my green outfit. The red shoes were last. "I won't need these. My quest is done." I choked on a sob, as I handed the shoes to Princess Ardis. I shoved my feet in my own shoes and tears splashed onto the laces as I tied them.

Queen Doris frowned and coughed. "Well now. This is certainly a predicament. If it weren't for the mix up with the crown, you would be safe at home. Hmm."

I wiped my hand across my eyes and turned to Prince Alex. "Here is your backpack."

He picked it up. "Thanks."

Princess Ardis tapped at the toes of the red shoes and they shrunk down to fairy size. She tied them to a belt at her waist. "I'm sorry, David. I don't think fairy dust can help you, either. It doesn't have enough power to go against the Permanence Effect." She flew over to me and kissed my cheek. "You can stay with us, too, you know."

"Thanks." I sighed.

"David, I have an idea. It's never been done, but it might work." Queen Doris took the crown from the safe and set it on the table. It glowed and pulsed.

A holographic image of a Drainosaur appeared. "What is the current need?"

Everyone gasped.

Queen Doris stepped closer to the image. "Old One, we have an ally, who has restored our crown. But in doing so has imperiled his own life. Because of the Permanence Effect, he must remain here. David is a topsider. Can you help us get him back to his home, learned Old One?"

Lights flashed and colors swirled around the room. A crackling noise grew louder and my ears felt like they were going to pop. Then everything went quiet and dark.

"It is done," a deep voice boomed. "Return to the proper door. Take care and thank you."

Lights came back on. Everyone looked at Queen Doris.

"Well, David, I see it is quarter to twelve. We have fifteen minutes to get you to the door in Drain Pipe One. Say goodbye and let's hurry!" Queen Doris smiled at me.

"Okay." I nodded, grinning and wiping the tears from my face. I stood and turned to the group in front of me. "Thank you for everything. I'll come back to visit, but now I must go home."

Oliver swaggered up to me. "Sure, rescue me and leave. You better come back." He wiped his eye with a swipe of his tail.

"I will. I promise. You can come and visit me, too." I hugged the little ferret. "Prince Alex and King Thomas, you always wanted to go topside. You'll be able to now."

"David, perhaps we will visit you." King Thomas and Alex took turns shaking my hand.

Queen Doris handed me the green bean hat. "We must put you on a door and fly you to the drain gateway where you entered. Then wear this and think of home. You will be there before you know it. And thank you for finding our crown. You are welcome here anytime."

CHAPTER 30

WE walked out of the palace into the cool night. A soft lemony breeze blew through my hair, as I put on the hat.

Gert and Trudy landed beside me. They waggled their gold speckled purple wings and giggled. "David, we just saw the funniest sight. A bunch of Marsh Fellows are playing leapfrog in the meadow."

Trudy chuckled. "The way they're hopping, it won't be long before they're back in the reeds by their home. They've got a few Drainosaurs playing, too."

"But they don't look very happy," said Gert. She pointed a foot at me. "Where are you going?"

"It's time for me to go back home. Can you fly me to the door in Drain Pipe One?" I pointed to a tall narrow pipe in the distance. A large neon number one lit up its side.

"Hop on. We'd be glad to," said Gert and Trudy together.

Smiling, I climbed onto Gert and Trudy and waved to the crowd as we flew away. Nearing the pipe, I spotted the door. A bell hung beside it with the sign *Ring for Service*. I tugged on a rope to ring it.

The door lowered like a drawbridge. "Enter carefully," a mechanical voice said.

I stepped down onto the metal surface and walked inside the pipe. Turning to Trudy and Gert, I saluted them. "Thank you. I'm so glad you've become such a beautiful Psychedelic Butterfly. Take care of yourselves."

Trudy wiped her nose with one of her feet. "Come back to see us, David. We'll have a Plumberry pie just for you."

I laughed. "Good. As long as I don't have to go to Trollsylvania for the plumberries. Bye." I stepped in further and let the door close.

In a corner I saw a pile of vegetable-shaped hats like the one I wore.

Clutching the velvet bag with Mama's ring, I squeezed my eyes shut. I thought of home, of Mama, and of Luis. Colors swirled in my mind as wind whooshed in my face.

The next thing I knew I was normal size, sitting in the kitchen sink.

My brother ran into the kitchen, letting the door slam behind him. "David, did you get Mama's ring back? If not, I'm gonna tell," he chanted in a sing-song voice. Then he pointed at my head. "Yuck! What's that green thing?"

"A hat. Yes, I got Mama's ring." I slid off the counter onto the floor. Opening the velvet bag, I felt around until I pulled out the now normal-size ring. I carefully set it on the ring dish.

"Phew! Lucky you. Mama's home and wants us to go to the store with her. Hurry up. We're out in the car." Luis ran back out the door.

I looked at the clock. Had time almost stood still? Just a few minutes had passed since Mama's ring had landed in the drain. I shook my head in disbelief. Luis looked like he'd stayed out of trouble too.

What a relief!

Taking off the green bean hat, I ran to my room and hid it in the top drawer under my socks. There, for another day. I put the velvet bag under the socks, too. Now, I just wanted to see Mama. Maybe later, I'd play baseball with Luis.

I ran outside, slamming the kitchen door behind me.

The End

About the Author

Janyce Brawn is a retired K-12 English as a Second Language and Spanish teacher who also has a degree in Art. She uses her art training to illustrate magazines and books. With a vivid imagination, Janyce has been writing and drawing since she was a little girl working on handwritten stories and crayoned pictures for books with her twin sister. Married to her husband for many amazing years, she has three grown sons, a daughter-in-law, and one granddaughter. Janyce has used her son's exploits for inspiration in her writing and art projects over the years. Her Boston Terrier is always curious about what she's doing at her desk and sticks her short nose into everything, thinking she is helping create characters and scenes. When Janyce isn't writing or drawing, she likes to read, go boating on the nearby lake, or visit with family and friends.

Made in the USA
Monee, IL
08 May 2021